Guardian Cats

& the Lost Books of Alexandria

Rahma Krambo

Reflected Light Books

Cover Design: Jamila Diallo
Cover Image: Laurie L. Snidow
Title page image: Wikipedia Commons Ancientlibraryalex.jpg

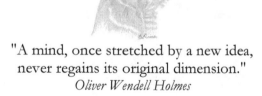

"A mind, once stretched by a new idea,
never regains its original dimension."
Oliver Wendell Holmes

Dedicated to
the two cats who started it all,
my friends who believed this was possible,
A.K. and J.D. who contributed
their unique vision and inspiration
and
to librarians everywhere.

MOONLIGHT AND PRINTER'S INK

Marco stayed up until dawn, the night he discovered he could read. He never dared think the books would speak to him like they did for Lucy. He had been content to curl up next to her in the library, listening. At first the sound of her voice drew him in, but gradually he grew to love the stories.

Then one night, Lucy left a book open on the window seat where the bright light of a full moon illuminated the page. Marco cocked his head, wondering if his eyes were playing tricks. The rows of black lines wavered as moonlight caused the paper to ripple, as if touched by a celestial finger.

Marco could not have known about the mystical effect of a full moon on cats and books left on their own in the library. Not until he saw the lines breathe, the words unveiled.

His heart pounded when he realized that Lucy's stories had been locked inside the books! And now he had the key!

His immediate surroundings, the rich scents of the library, mahogany, leather and brocade, receded into the background. He no longer heard the grandfather clock's steady ticking. Time stood still while moonlight and printer's ink transported him and four children through an English wardrobe to a place of everlasting winter. There, a majestic lion befriended them and liberated his kingdom from the spell of an evil witch.

He was hooked. He couldn't wait to open another book. He inspected the shelves with the knowledge that books were no longer the unique property of humans. They were, like the wardrobe in the story, a portal which opened into strange and wonderful places.

And now he held a magical pass.

Where would these other books take him? And where in the world would he start? There were so many to choose from. That night he did not sleep a wink. Each one transported him into a new adventure. How amazing, he thought, that books, once opened, were so much bigger on the inside.

In the wee hours of the night, Marco became a warrior, a wizard, a wanderer, but he was always the hero. When Marco read, he forgot he was a cat.

A FORCE TO BE RECKONED WITH

The nights stretched out longer and colder, each one stealing warmth and light from the previous day. Marco didn't mind. It gave him more time to read.

In the early evenings, Lucy and her grandmother played cards or watched TV in the living room. In the company of a crackling fire they sipped hot tea, and Marco had his choice of two warm laps.

Later, while Lucy and her grandma slept, Marco settled into the library and read. His armchair travels took him to exotic places full of adventure, intrigue and danger. He had a perfect life.

Many adventures passed and the days gradually outstretched the nights, until one morning the clamor of song birds shattered the chill of winter. Marco stretched and yawned. The library glowed with warm sunlight diffused through gauzy under curtains. All around him books were scattered about, and he hoped Lucy wouldn't scold him too much.

No matter, he thought, then curled up on the leather ottoman and fell asleep. He dreamed of being in a clearing in the woods. An enormous hawk took off from atop a tree, swooped down in a wide circle and Marco was suddenly flying—the hawk's wings spread wide on both sides, almost as if they were his. Wind whooshing, flattening his ears, Marco was exhilarated, soaring high above the ground, when the bird suddenly turned and they were no longer in a sunny meadow, but a dark alley between buildings.

Together they made the descent—plummeting downward toward an unlit brick street with a single car parked in the shadows. At the last moment, Marco saw the man. He was frantically trying to unlock the car door. The hawk shrieked—just before striking the man to the ground.

Marco was startled out of his dream; the hawk's piercing call still in his ears. But the sound didn't go away. The shrill cry was no dream! He jumped down from the ottoman and fought the urge to run.

This was a force to be reckoned with, right? Just the kind of thing that might require the services of a hero. That ruled out ducking under the bed.

The clamor was coming from outside, so it was possible the threat could pass. He chose the writing desk beneath a library window as his vantage point and poked his nose through the sheer curtains. Screeching to a halt in front of the house was an extraordinary vehicle flashing beams of red and blue light from its top.

What a strange creature, he thought. Its cries abruptly ceased and the back end of its white shell burst open, casting two men from inside. Like prisoners escaping, they ran at full speed towards the house.

Were they friend or foe? Were they on a rescue mission or was Marco's house under attack? And how in the world do you tell the difference? He didn't realize being a hero required so many decisions.

Lucy ran past the library towards the front door and, in what seemed to him like a reckless moment, threw the house wide open to total strangers. She turned and dashed toward the back while the men chased after her.

Marco pursued them as they rushed towards Grandma's room. But tailing him from behind was a metal bed on squeaky wheels, and one of the men pushing it booted Marco in the head.

His ears rang from the blow and he ducked under the chaise lounge at the end of the hallway to regroup. How would he save Lucy and her grandma from these men who had obviously come to abduct them?

How did heroes in books always seem to know the right thing to do?

He tried to stay calm. He knew a hero must look danger square in the eye and take action. Hunkered down under the chaise lounge, he was trying to come up with a plan when the ear-splitting jangle of a telephone overhead broke his resolve. He made his getaway, finding refuge on a bookshelf. He was so mortified at his failed rescue mission, he refused to budge even when Lucy called his name.

After a long silence, Marco emerged from his hiding place. The desolation of an empty house was overwhelming. It had always been peopled. Lucy, her friends. The cook, the nurse, and the gardener.

He sat on the writing desk, looking out the front window into the fading light. How could he face the fact that his humans had been kidnapped and he had done nothing to save them? He went upstairs to Lucy's room, hoping for a miracle. Maybe she disappeared through the back of her closet, like the one in the book, he thought with a burst of optimism. But no, the wall was solid and the only thing left of Lucy was her scent. For two days, he mewed inside the vacant house and nibbled on diminishing crumbs in his food bowl.

Empty space eventually fills up with something. A void, cultivated in the aftermath of misfortune, begins to attract the wrong kind of attention. Marco knew it was time to leave when disagreeable spirits started roaming freely through the house, as if they owned the place.

On the third day he stood at the front door, which the spirits must have left open. He stared out at the clouds while they moved and stretched across the sky.

It looked so big out there. He poked his nose through the door and sniffed the air. What in the world would he do outside?

BOOK OF THE DEAD

Leo Chin held the door open for a woman and her daughter while he collapsed his umbrella into a refined black walking stick and entered the Great Court of the British Museum.

As curator of Egyptian Rare Book Archives, he could have gone into the complex closer to his office, but he never tired of passing through the museum, breathing the air of ancient things. The current exhibit in the Reading Room's enormous rotunda featured the *Book of the Dead*, instructions for an ancient Egyptian's afterlife.

He was in front of the papyrus that contained a spell for help in the weighing of the heart when Arthur Nightingale, assistant curator of Roman and Egyptian Antiquities, came to stand beside him.

"What do you think, Professor Chin?"

"Superb as usual. The museum has outdone itself once again."

"I meant the Egyptian's view of death," Arthur said. "They were lucky to have such potent spells to protect them in their night journey."

"Knowledge is a powerful thing," Professor Chin replied.

"A little magic doesn't hurt either, does it?" quipped Arthur. He patted the breast and side pockets of his jacket, looking for something. "Do you suppose they'd work for an Englishman?"

The corners of Professor Chin's mouth stretched into a smile. He was glad Arthur thought of him as an Englishman. "If you had enough money. Only the rich can afford to die properly, even now."

"Yes, well…" Arthur's cell phone vibrated with an incoming call. "That's Croner. I have a meeting. Best be off. Good day Professor.

"Good day to you."

Professor Chin wound his way through the Museum's labyrinthine corridors to his department. Just as he got to his office which, was little more than a cubicle, his assistant, Oliver, approached him.

"I made your flight reservations, Professor. You'll be leaving on the ninth, a day ahead of the conference, with the layover in Greece as you requested."

"Very good. Thank you, Oliver."

He entered a tiny but well-ordered world. Piles of books were everywhere, but he knew the exact location of each one. He hung his umbrella and coat and removed his fedora. On the desk was yesterday's unsorted mail. It was the usual—catalogues, book review and trade journals—but when he picked up the stack, a postcard fell to the floor.

Professor Chin froze. The picture side was splashed with the gaudy colors of the Romanian flag and two dancing gypsies. He picked it up and looked on the other side. It had been forwarded twice.

"Leo, why don't you write? We never hear from you and wonder if you died. Your poor mother is rolling over in her grave, worried sick about what's become of you. Serves her right for marrying that horrible Gaje. You are full-blooded. Never forget!

Have you gotten married yet? Please, everyone here is dying of curiosty."

It was no surprise his illiterate aunt had misspelled curiosity. Why couldn't she leave him alone? His stomach knotted and he dropped into his chair.

"You've come a long way," said a voice from an unlit corner of the room.

"You're still here?" asked Professor Chin.

"Of course," said the voice.

"Why?"

"You still need me."

"Most people leave their imaginary friends at home when they grow up."

"You're not 'most people'. And I'm not imaginary. I was your only true friend when you had none; when you were tormented by your own family and the outsiders; when your father beat you for trying to protect your mother. You needed me then and you need me now."

Professor Chin sighed and surrendered to his lifelong companion. There was no use fighting it. He would never be a true *Gaje*, a non-gypsy, but he would certainly never return to 'his people'. He had no family, no home, no country.

But he still had dreams, and there were others like him. Together, he hoped, they would create a world of their own.

"If you want your dreams to be real," the Whisperer said, "you will need more powerful magic. Your fortune telling mother was right. You have the Gift. But you need more than herbs, runes and rituals to accomplish your dreams."

STRAY CATS AND CASTLES

Next to the dumpster behind a gas station, Marco found food. Hardly the tuna or crunchy nuggets he was used to, but he was in no position to complain. Gas fumes mixed with the rancid odor of rotting garbage, but his belly had been rumbling for days and he gobbled up the meager pickings. It made him even hungrier.

The smell of meat drew him to search at the back of the trash bin. His head was caught in a tight space when he heard someone behind him.

"Punk! Did I say you could eat here?"

Marco involuntarily jerked his head up, but he only succeeded in getting more stuck.

"What a cretin," said the voice. Another voice chimed in, and Marco learned a few words he'd never read in books. He was so humiliated, he considered staying stuck, in hopes they might give up and go away. He tried crawling farther in, but to his dismay he was suddenly free.

Free to face the cats who had been cursing him behind his back. They were practically in his face and he was trapped by the dumpster and a brick wall.

"Did you find what you were looking for?"

"Uh… no."

"Uh… right. You sound like a smart guy. Where you from, stranger?"

Marco had the feeling that whatever he said was going to be the wrong answer. Besides, he didn't know where he was from anymore.

"I'm from…" Marco looked off vaguely in the direction of his old neighborhood.

"He looks lost, like a pet. Don't you think?"

"I'm not…"

"Then you gots to be a stray. Like us!" said the smallest one.

What a horrifying thought. Was he a stray? Was this what his future looked like?

"This is our turf, runt. And there's barely enough food for us. So scram."

Marco was only too glad to leave the ragtag cats to their smelly dumpster and he took the opportunity to bolt.

"What a wuss. You're not gonna last long out here! Pet!" the cats called out behind him.

Marco trotted along deserted sun-baked sidewalks, glad to have escaped the street cats, but the heat was searing his tender toe pads. Life on the outside was harsh. He was always hungry and thirsty, and he had no training in the hunt. Now he discovered he had enemies he didn't even know existed. Some hero he was turning out to be. He couldn't even defend himself against a few alley cats.

He longed for a place to rest, but he was surrounded by dry scrub and empty lots. Something made him lift his head, though, and look farther in the distance.

As if by magic, the promise of relief appeared. He quickened his pace until he reached the cool shade of buildings and green leafy trees that seemed to grow out of the sidewalks.

His spirits raised, he explored the streets and found a puddle of water to quench his thirst. A girl patted him on his head before she disappeared through one of the shop doors.

At the end of one street was a stone building nestled in a grove of trees. A dome sprouted from the roof, and the rounded turrets at both corners reminded him of a castle, like ones he'd seen in books.

On one side was a good climbing tree, which beckoned him to climb into its cool arms. It held him like an old friend and he curled up on a wide branch that fit comfortably. It was the perfect napping place. He fell asleep the moment he closed his eyes.

How could such an ideal napping spot bring on such a terrifying dream?

Marco was surrounded by complete darkness, the lack of light so dense it had substance, like an invisible creature. Had he been eaten by a predator? He panicked, thrashing out in all directions, but it was impossible to fight an enemy he couldn't see.

Somehow the realization came... who this enemy was. He understood that it was fear, his own fear.

A force welled up inside him, moving up into his throat and out of his mouth. He bellowed... like a lion, shattering chains he didn't know were there. He would not go down like this! Before he sprang, he recoiled and roared

13

again; something terrible and savage in a voice he did not recognize as his own.

OLD PAPER, LEATHER AND INK

Marco awoke, startled to find he was still in the tree, as though nothing had happened. The dream evaporated like mist, and the sun, low and bold, glowed briefly through the canopy of magnolia leaves before disappearing altogether.

It was his favorite time of day, this fading light that heralded the coming of night. The atmosphere shifted with a quality that came in the natural order of things, like the phases of the moon or the changing of the guard.

A slight breeze kicked up and the leaves of the magnolia tree waved at him, inviting him to play. He climbed to where tree and roof entwined from years of companionship, pressing his way through the thick foliage until he reached open sky.

The town, spread out below in a carpet of trees and buildings, was threaded by a river and bordered by distant hills. This must be the top of the world, he thought. Only the church spire reached higher into the sky, and he felt immensely happy for the first time since he'd been on his own. Nothing lifted his spirits quite like a good view.

Lights blinked on across the town, and he made a game of trying to guess where the next one would appear, but he couldn't keep up. He got up to explore a large dome on the ridge of the roof. Banded with small windows all around, through one pane of glass, another cat looked straight back at him.

Marco searched for a way in and found a broken window worked as well as any door.

The air inside was musty, and he recognized the earthy scent of old books. Without stopping to think, he jumped in, expecting to land on the floor. But the dome windows were designed for letting in light, not cats, and Marco was suddenly hanging by his claws on a narrow piece of wood.

He made the mistake of looking down, lost his grip and plummeted towards the ground. A wooden beam broke his fall and from there, he leaped to the top of a bookshelf, unsettling small puffs of ancient dust. As he descended to the floor, he breathed in the rich scent of old paper, leather and ink and the promise of countless stories.

The silence was made deeper by the steady ticking of the grandfather clock. But there was something hiding within—he could feel it—and he moved with stealth through his new surroundings, alert for any sign of danger.

His ears perked up as he caught a quick spatter of voices.

Cautiously, he approached the stacks. The voices spoke, muffled and intermittent, as though waking from a long nap.

Marco could not resist eavesdropping, no matter the risk, and followed them right into one of the dark hollows, its walls made entirely of books. Like vendors calling out their wares, the books began making their pitch.

"I never knew a trail to get cold so quickly," came a gruff voice from one book.

"Let us carry Sir Gill's body in honor from the battlefield, lest he be trampled by the horses." That voice came from a different one.

"If Mr. Boswell shot himself," a mystery book argued, "there would be powder marks around the wound."

Further on, a woman screamed, a man shouted, and he heard the clip clop of horse hoofs on brick.

"They are dragging her away!"

A clank of metal. "Good! My sword is at my side. I will defend her at all costs."

Talking books sure made it easier to find something to read, thought Marco, as he pawed *The Three Musketeers* off the shelf and settled down on the floor. He liked the hero, d'Artagnan, and as he read, he forgot he was a cat. He became d'Artagnan, rescued several fair maidens, fought evil and injustice, and shrugged off danger as if it were a game.

In the middle of a duel, a faint sound, like the tinkling of bells, broke the story's spell. He lost his concentration, left d'Artagnan on his own and got up to investigate. A soft rush of air and a wave of motion passed through his body, like the flutter of angel wings. He followed the rustling of energy as though it beckoned to him. What kind of books might possibly be on the second floor?

THE OLD LIBRARY CAT

At the top of the stairs, the sound of pages turning and a deep, almost human sigh drew Marco toward the farthermost row of shelves. They hid a wall of doors, all closed except for the last. Through the crack in the door, he saw a wall of books leaning against each other like old men.

Marco moved into the doorway. On a long table sat a cat. Not the same as the one in the window. This one, larger and silver-spotted, was hunched over a book. All around him were stacks of books, and he seemed not to notice anything except what he was reading. His tail, laid out to the side, quivered in annoyance.

Marco stood spellbound, half-in, half-out of the room. A soft light moved about, illuminating dust motes and causing shadows to ebb and flow like waves.

Bang! A massive book hit the floor like a gunshot, and Marco jumped a foot off the ground. The room darkened and the grandfather clock downstairs pealed off twelve counts of midnight.

Marco's heart raced. He stared in wonder at the other cat, who continued his studies as though nothing out of the ordinary had happened.

Marco took a deep breath and chanced a step closer to the elder cat, who remained arched over his book. He crept in, tilting his head to try and read the titles. Something about an atom, another book about visible and invisible light, and one called The Double Slit Experiment.

It was obvious this cat did not want to be disturbed, so Marco decided to leave. But he turned too quickly, misjudging the placement of the door, and thudded against it.

With a disgruntled sigh, the scholarly cat looked up. "What is it? What do you want?"

Marco dearly wished he'd stayed downstairs.

"Speak up. What are you looking for?"

"I'm... I'm not sure what I'm looking for," said Marco.

"Then how will you know when you find it?"

His mind went blank; he was ready to bolt.

The older cat left his book, his tone softening. "I see you are enjoying The Three Musketeers."

Marco halted in his tracks. "Well... yes," he replied. Books were one thing Marco could talk about, and now that he had something to say, he lost some of his shyness.

He started to ramble on about the story, then caught himself, remembering the strange titles this cat had been reading. He wouldn't be much interested in Marco's adventure stories.

"I didn't know other cats could read," said Marco. "I thought I was the only one."

"There is much you do not know, young Marco."

"How do you know my name?" he asked, and then realized he hadn't told him what book he was reading, either. How had he known?

The old cat ignored his question. "D'Artagnan is waiting for you to come back and give him his voice. The characters are like that sometimes. If they find a reader they like, they freeze until the reader releases them."

Marco felt deep in his bones that he had already known that, but he didn't realize he knew until now.

The old cat jumped to the floor and came toward him, limping slightly.

"My name is Cicero," he said. "I am glad to make your acquaintance. Reader cats are a rare breed these days."

Marco had no memory of meeting Cicero before, but there was something familiar about him.

Cicero looked directly into Marco's eyes. "If you would like to learn more, come again tomorrow night."

Cicero was odd, but Marco was curious and the old cat didn't seem dangerous. "I'll be back," Marco said and turned to leave.

He was already out the door when Cicero called out. "The storeroom on the other side... the window's always open."

Marco realized Cicero had given him directions for getting out of the library. When he turned back to give him a nod of thanks, however, the elder cat had vanished.

NARROW ESCAPES

Marco squeezed through the narrow opening in the window to find the magnolia tree waiting. He made note of this handy arrangement, glad he wouldn't have to fall through the roof to get back into the library.

He trotted off down the street in good spirits. All he needed was a safe place to sleep until morning. A house where the owner kept cat food on the porch would be especially nice. Oh, and a cushioned chair. He nosed around porches and back yards in his quest for the perfect spot.

Sounds of soft rolling drums in the distance announced a coming storm. The smell of impending rain flavored the scent of dry food wafting between the cracks of a board fence, and his stomach growled a fierce reminder of his neglect. The fence was a lot trickier to climb than a tree, but hunger drove him to success, and he perched for a moment on the top rail to view the lightning flashes. Better hurry before the rain starts, he thought.

That's when Marco discovered a creature more deadly than stray cats. Without warning, a beast of a dog, the size of twenty cats, smacked against the inside of the fence. The dog jumped up again and again, like his hind legs were made of springs, his fangs slathered with drool.

Marco had never been somebody's prey. He dug his claws into the narrow rail, his destiny teetering in the imbalance of the wobbly fence. On one of his jumps, the dog's teeth sank into Marco's tail, and his fate seemed to edge towards a grisly death. The dog lost his grip on Marco's slender tail and there was a moment of blessed silence.

Before Marco could start breathing again, however, the dog returned, with renewed vigor. When the dog's razor-sharp teeth nipped at his hind leg, Marco's survival instincts kicked in. His powerful hind legs pushed him off the fence, like a swimmer soaring off a diving board.

He flew into the air. Not high, but high enough. His body spiraled and arched into a perfect back flip achieved only by felines and practiced gymnasts, and he made a four-point landing on the safe side of the fence. The dog clawed and barked stupidly on the other side.

Marco didn't stop running until he reached the safety of a tree. For a long time his heart pounded so hard, he barely heard the thunder. He only noticed when it stopped and the lightning made a brilliant show, turning night into day. Who would guess its delicate beauty masked its true purpose? How could he know beforehand that the lightning was a warning?

Then thunder cracked its whip, sounding like the world had split in two, and Marco almost fell off the wide branch. He scrambled back up and held on while the skies opened and let everything loose.

Even though Marco had seen rain before, it had been from inside a house, protected by windows. A thick cover of green foliage, which might have sheltered him during a light shower, was taking a beating too, and Marco finished out the night hunched on the branch, wet and shivering, trying to endure.

When dawn finally arrived, the storm lumbered off like a beast seeking the cover of darkness. Marco felt like a sailor, lost at sea. I'm shipwrecked, he thought, wishing he'd finished the book about the sailor so he knew how the story turned out.

The sun appeared and the sky cleared to a brilliant blue, but Marco was determined to stay gloomy. A gust of wind stirred the damp leaves and shook water droplets onto his already soggy fur, which helped justify his mood. That, and the flock of crows that landed in the tree.

Their raucous cawing was the final straw. Marco picked his way to the ground and found a sunny patch of sidewalk, where he started grooming his fur. When he was a little drier, he set off to look for something to eat, still feeling sorry for himself.

"I'm too young to die!"

Marco heard the cry for help, but saw no one.

"Help! Get me outa here!" At the corner of the house, a pipe ran top to bottom, out of which protruded a bushy wiggling tail. Marco pawed it.

"Cut that out!" The invisible creature squealed and struggled inside his enclosure.

Marco had all kinds of questions, but the biggest one involved helping. What could he possibly do? He tried poking his paw inside the pipe, but it agitated the creature more. He scratched at a loose section and got his claw wedged in between the metal strapping and pipe. Now he was stuck. He yanked and pulled until the metal band broke loose from its fastener, freeing Marco. He was licking his wounded paw when the whole pipe split open like a cotton pod and out spilled a creature like nothing he'd ever seen before.

Poor thing doesn't have any ears, was his first thought. The long willowy creature dashed off like he was leaving, then ducked and rolled into a somersault and came hurtling back towards Marco. He screeched to a full stop and pressed his nose into Marco's face.

"You saved my life! You're my hero!"

"I didn't really do…"

"Man, I thought I was going to die!" He took off running, then came back chattering nonsense and swooped over Marco, nuzzling him like they were old buddies.

"I'm freeeeee!"

Marco was stunned.

"Hey, you're kind of fat for a ferret, aren't you?"

"A ferret?" said Marco. "What's a ferret?"

"I'm a ferret!" the creature declared, bobbing and arching across the lawn like something made of rubber and springs.

The ferret looped his way back. "Hey, you're awfully quiet. What's your name? I'm Polo. You wanna see my treasure chest?" He didn't wait for an answer and disappeared into a hole under the house.

Marco peered inside, letting his eyes adjust to the dim light. The ferret was bounding around the small space.

"Stay close to me or you might get lost," he said and disappeared again.

Marco followed, across wooden beams, around metal pipes and over cardboard boxes. When the ferret reached his destination, he stood upright with his arm pointing to a pile of rubbish. "Tada!" he announced in a grand voice.

Marco walked over to the pile and sniffed.

"Isn't it great? Hey, I got something I want to show you. Where is it now?" He looked around and then dove into and out of the clothes, sometimes buried and sometimes emerging, just to disappear again seconds later. When his head finally popped up, he had a gold bracelet in his mouth.

"Cooo..huh?" Polo dropped the bracelet. "I shouldn't talk with my mouth full. Me mum always told me that, but sometimes I forget."

Marco moved among the piles of clothes and gadgets, mystified by the ferret's enthusiasm. Some treasure. What kind of creature collects trash and calls it treasure?

Polo sprang to within an inch of his face. "Hey, I just had an idea. We could be a team. You and me. Wouldn't that be fun! You'll be the lookout."

As strange as he was, Polo's company cheered him immensely. He was, by a long shot, friendlier than anyone he'd met on the streets. Maybe things were looking up.

Then the little creature suddenly collapsed in a twisted heap and Marco dashed over, nudging the ferret to see if he was dead.

NIGHT WATCH

Cicero's room was filled with books, old favorites like Shakespeare, biographies of great men, and the more challenging ones about quantum physics. Their presence filled him with peace, like old friends who read together, not needing to hold meaningless conversations.

Cicero arose and stretched his front legs out on the table where he was reading a book by a man named Einstein. It was time for his regular night watch of the library, not that there was much to lose sleep over in all the years he'd been here. No one would ever find him or the Book in this sleepy little town. But the stiffness in his old bones wouldn't let him forget he was going to need a successor soon.

Out on the balcony, Cicero overlooked his domain. He had grown very fond of the Angel Springs library, even though circumstances for his transfer here were made under duress. Except for the ticking of the grandfather clock, all was quiet. In the darkened library there was only the soft glow of a large aquarium in the children's area.

Cicero's ears perked up at the sound of pages turning. Had the young cat returned as promised? It was critical Marco had kept his word about returning tonight, but Cicero was used to broken promises. He tried to contain his hopes as he searched the first floor and found Marco lost in a book.

The young cat didn't even notice his presence and Cicero fought the impulse of making a rash decision. He did not want to make the same mistake again, but there was something about Marco. Something besides his choice of reading material and long tail, a sure sign of intelligence.

He had to remind himself that intelligence was only one aspect needed to be a Guardian. Wasn't it his own reverence for knowledge that had blinded him before? Hadn't he learned how deceiving appearances could be?

Marco's slender tail twitched. He was young; all the better for training, but youthfulness had its drawbacks. The vulnerability of youth could be heartbreaking. Cicero sighed. He had enough worries. Why did he always want to add more?

Then he winced. He was getting way ahead of himself. He barely knew Marco. And why on earth did he think it was only the young who were victims of deceit?

Cicero gave himself a good scratching to shake off his fears and exchanged his gloomy thoughts for the cheerful anticipation of a visit to his old friend Akeel. It must certainly be no accident that Marco showed up at this critical time. If destiny was working in his favor, he would have a traveling companion.

To Marco, he said, "I see you are reading about your namesake."

Marco jumped a little, startled by Cicero's sudden appearance.

"Yes," he replied. "I... I mean Marco Polo... was being introduced to the Mongol emperor."

"You enjoy a good adventure," said Cicero, in a way that could have been either a statement or a question.

"Yes," Marco answered, flustered by Cicero's gaze. He had questions. Like how did the adventurer get two names? And what did it mean that he and Polo shared the name of this famous explorer?

But he didn't ask. The look in Cicero's eyes stopped him.

"You are free to continue reading about the adventures of others," said Cicero. "Remain among these common books." He spoke in such an odd way, as though he were giving and taking something at the same time.

Marco held his breath.

"But I must counsel you," continued Cicero. "There are worlds far beyond your ordinary imagination, far beyond what you find here." With that, Cicero turned and headed for the stairs. He paused but did not bother to glance back. "Tonight, you must make a choice. Stay with your safe adventure stories," he said as he climbed the stairs. "Others' adventures, I should say..."

Marco felt light headed, then remembered to breathe.

"...or follow me, young Marco Polo, on a true adventure." Cicero continued up the staircase, in no way resembling heroes Marco met in books. But even when he could no longer be seen, Cicero left a trail of powerful energy in the room.

He tried to shake off the spell, and when he finally did, he was a little offended by Cicero's remark. Safe? Who does he think he is? And just what is wrong with my imagination?

Marco was getting a little indignant. I travel throughout the human world in their books. Sometimes I even forget I am a cat. What's safe about my adventures?

He scrunched over his book, but he'd lost his place and couldn't remember what had been happening anyway. His thoughts were muddled and the air was filled with an electric charge. Even though he tried ignoring it, curiosity grabbed hold of him. Cicero was bigger than he looked, thought Marco, and then wondered what in the world that meant.

When Marco entered Cicero's chambers, the old cat was curled up, sleeping on a long wooden table. His eyes were still closed when he said, "Come in. I'm just resting up for our journey."

The Last Peaceful Moment

'What journey?' wondered Marco. He thought Cicero wanted to show him a book. What other kind of adventure would be in the library?

"Do you believe in destiny?"

Marco had no idea what destiny was, but he wasn't about to admit it. He chanced an answer. "Sure."

"Good. Because I think it is no mistake, your coming here. Especially tonight." Cicero jumped down from the table and peered deep into Marco's eyes. "By the way, how did you learn to read?"

Marco backed up from the intensity of Cicero's gaze. "It… it was a girl. I don't know if she was intending to. One night, the words started making sense on their own. But it was Lucy who read aloud to me at first."

"Human transmission. Interesting. Reading is normally passed down from one of your elders." Cicero paced the length of the table. From a high place, a warm glow appeared. Marco sat on the floor, feeling small and insignificant.

"I want to show you a book. A book that is both here and not here."

The warm glow strayed from its position, causing Cicero's shadow to shift and leap onto a wall of books. He looked larger than life in that dark, book-cluttered room.

"But I'm afraid I must delay your introduction to the Book, because there is a human I want you to meet first."

Then, as if there was no question about it, Cicero said, "Come."

Spellbound, Marco followed him down to the library's main floor, up onto an antique hutch that held a display of classic children's books. They were staring at their images in a mirror.

Marco thought this must be routine behavior for a library cat, but he found it disturbing to look at the 'ghost cat' in the mirror. He squirmed.

"Be still," Cicero instructed. "This will be a different kind of traveling. From here on out, be prepared for anything. Things are not always as they appear. This mirror, for instance."

Cicero and his mirror twin nodded towards the floating light that had followed along and their images vanished. Then the mirror vanished, leaving a gaping black hole which Cicero walked through, as though it were something he did every night.

Marco sniffed the edges of where the mirror had been. He was cautious about going through doors, especially ones which magically appeared out of nowhere. He looked for evidence of the vanished mirror and found none. But Cicero had disappeared and his curiosity pushed him onwards. He gingerly stepped through the frame into the darkness.

Nothing was the same on the other side. He was in a narrow passageway with rock walls, like a cave. Cold stone steps led downwards into more darkness. He peered into the hollow blackness and fought a sense of panic. The opening he had passed through had closed. Marco was trapped.

Cicero called up from below, a bodiless voice in the void. "Don't be afraid. Think of it as an adventure."

Marco took the first step. This didn't seem like adventures he read about in books. There was no enemy, nothing to fight against. No swords, no pirates. Only the soft bouncing light and his jagged shadow on the rock wall accompanied his descent.

When he reached a platform, the walls on one side dropped away. They were in a deep cavern, even darker and more boundless than the stairways.

But Cicero wasn't looking out through the railing into the cavern. Marco turned to face the rock wall and found there was a door, just a regular door. For some reason, this small bit of familiarity comforted Marco.

The door creaked open. The floating light led the way, and this time Marco did not hesitate to follow.

The room was nothing more than a small cave. Marco explored its nooks and crannies while Cicero waited, but the room was occupied only by a single wooden table. Why did Cicero bring him to such a strange place? He jumped up to join Cicero on the table and saw what he couldn't see from the floor.

"You must not tell anyone about this," Cicero said.

What was there to tell? There was a box. Sitting on a table. It smelled nice but that was about it.

"Don't think that this is an ordinary box," Cicero said. "Why do you think it is hidden in such a place?" he asked, then answered his own question. "Only something of value needs this kind of protection."

Marco wondered what was in the box, but he didn't ask. Cicero seemed to be asking all the questions. "Do you know what a sentinel is?"

"Um…" Marco started, but had no answer.

"A sentinel is like… a soldier." Cicero paused, then smiled slightly and nodded. "A quiet soldier. Yes, I like that description," he said, obviously pleased with himself.

"Cats are sentinels…" he continued. "Foolish humans, the ones who don't understand us, think we do nothing but sleep. What they do not know…" his voice trailed off. "They are a full time job, this responsibility of human caretaking."

Marco didn't know it, but this wouldn't be the last time Cicero would ramble on about his theory of humans and other favorite topics.

"They are well disposed—humans who take us for a friend. We are ever alert, even when we appear to be napping. We do not sleep in the manner of dogs. Our ears are attuned to frequencies beyond this world."

Marco wished Cicero would explain why they were so far underground, but Cicero wasn't through explaining other things.

"It was natural that we were chosen to be sentinels, or guardians of the books, as well. Not only ordinary books, but now... Now, I must show you the real reason why I am the library cat."

Cicero lowered his voice, even though no one was around. "I must take you on a journey. To another place. Another time. There you will meet the original Guardians."

Cicero brought his attention full onto Marco. "Are you ready?"

"Sure," agreed Marco. Cicero was eccentric, but he wasn't dangerous, like the alley cats, and Marco was curious to see where Cicero would take him.

"All right then. Close your eyes," Cicero directed. "And whatever you do, don't open them until we get there."

They were sitting on the table, like bookends, their noses close enough that Marco felt warm puffs of Cicero's breath. A soft humming stirred the air. He had to peek.

"Keep them closed!" ordered Cicero.

Marco slammed his eyes shut and tried to copy Cicero. He didn't know what to think about, so he pictured Lucy. Something fluttered above his head and the soft humming grew distant. Something was quivering, but it was hard to tell if it came from outside or inside of him.

"Alaniah, I believe we are ready," Cicero called out to the darkness.

Marco felt a tingling, then an odd sense of floating, as though he'd left his body. It was an unusual, but not unpleasant feeling. He wondered if they were on a boat, rocking on ocean waves. The rising and falling made him drowsy. It was the last peaceful moment of their trip.

FALLING THROUGH TIME

Without warning, a tremendous force grabbed hold and sucked Marco downward. He did not know he was in a vortex. All he knew was pain, like something was exploding inside his head. He opened his eyes to try to get his bearings, but that only made things worse. Light was rushing past him on all sides. Not just everyday light, but weird, all stretched-out-of-shape light, whizzing past like he was sitting in one place and the entire universe was in motion. His stomach lurched and he came close to throwing up.

Stop! He wanted to scream, but nothing came out of his twisted mouth. On and on he spun, falling and spinning faster than the speed of light. Then abruptly, as though he'd been propelled into a dark void, the noise stopped and he was floating. He saw nothing. He heard nothing, not even faintly, and he could not feel his body anymore.

I must be dead now, he thought with a strange calmness. In fact, he was deliriously happy. Even though he couldn't move, it didn't seem to matter.

Then life returned to his body. But life meant feelings. At first, there were just prickly sensations, but that quickly passed. His legs were trembling. Then his whole body shook and the shaking became tremors and soon his entire body convulsed out of control. The last thing he remembered was wishing he *were* dead.

THE SOUND OF THE SCRIBES

The gurgling, watery sounds were pleasant enough, but Marco was reluctant to open his eyes again. However, he couldn't resist a quick peek. There was a winged horse, frozen, but looking as though it were about to take flight. Marco supposed it wouldn't hurt to open his other eye. He was sitting on a stone wall surrounding a large pool of water. The winged horse was in the middle of the pool, and all around him sprays of sparkling water rose and fell. The sun shone as if it were a normal spring day.

Cicero sat on the wall next to him, licking his fur.

"Are we dead?" asked Marco.

"The first trip is the hardest. I told you not to open your eyes, but it's hard not to. Don't worry. It gets easier." Cicero was washing his tail. "It always takes me a while to recover."

The first trip? What was he talking about? And how could Cicero be so casual? Marco had enough. It was time for answers. "What did you do to me?" he demanded. "Are you trying to get me killed?"

Cicero continued grooming, and Marco thought he was avoiding the question because it might be true. What had he gotten himself into?

Cicero completed putting his fur in order and then they were both gazing at the winged horse who was reared back, his front legs pawing at the air. "Time traveling is always risky, and this trip is especially difficult," he began. "We had to come a long way to get back to the fourth century. Over sixteen centuries."

Marco had no clue what he was talking about.

"It's a bit challenging for your first trip, but it couldn't be helped. Then, of course, we had to move through space as well. When you add both aspects together like that... Well, you see, if we were simply traveling into another dimension, we could have used a portal. Those are easy, but one never knows where they'll end up. Portals are no good when you have to pinpoint an event."

Marco wondered how he was going to find his way home. He got up on all fours and almost fell into the pool.

"Give yourself time to adjust," said Cicero. "You'll be fine."

Marco sat back down. He surrendered for the moment and took to licking the fountain's mist from his fur while Cicero droned on in the background.

"There's no way to explain time travel. Even if you've read about folding space, wormholes, black and white holes, you'd have no better idea of what to expect. I've been studying for years and I still don't understand how it all works."

Marco thought a wormhole should be for worms, not cats. As for traveling, until now his longest journey had been to the town library. When he looked at Cicero, there was two of him. Clearly, things were not becoming clearer.

"You mean to tell me you don't understand how we got here?" asked Marco.

"I'm beginning to. But I wouldn't travel without a guide. We'd probably end up getting sucked into a black hole or stuck forever in some time warp, never to return."

This was hardly reassuring. "Then how *did* we get here?"

"I'm terribly sorry. You haven't met our guide yet, have you? Alaniah. She seems to have fluttered off somewhere. Visiting friends, most likely."

Marco looked around, beyond the fountain and his puzzling companion. There were flower gardens and more fountains. There were orange and lemon trees with benches under them. There were plenty of humans, all in strange dress. Most were reading. Maybe not so bad, he thought. "What is this place?"

"Ah, a question with an easy answer. Welcome to the Library of Alexandria."

"A library? It looks more like a park."

"Your vision is limited, Marco. Look further," said Cicero.

Marco stretched his neck. Buildings surrounded the gardens, enormous structures even from a distance.

"Which one is the library?" he asked, dazzled by the immensity.

"All of them. Every one is filled with books and scrolls, paintings and art."

"All of them?" he asked, wishing he didn't sound so daft.

"Come on, let's try out our legs." Cicero jumped down from the ledge and Marco followed, wobbly as a newborn kitten.

"Better to walk it off," Cicero said as he set off on the wide pathway.

They meandered through gardens, people watching. Some sat on benches, others sprawled on the grass. Some were reading and others sat at tables littered with books and tea cups, men animated by lively discussions.

Cicero explained as they walked. "This library was designed to be the greatest center of learning ever built, to be more than simply a building that stores books, but a place where humans would discuss the ideas in them. What a grand idea come to life!"

They passed a small gathering of people debating whether the earth was flat.

"They say there are over a half million books in dozens of languages here," Cicero continued.

Out of every people-cluster Marco passed, he heard snippets of spirited conversation about heaven and earth and various names—Copernicus, Hypatia, Ptolemy and Plato.

There were cats too. They sat on laps or under benches, but none of them paid any attention to them. After this leisurely stroll, Marco's legs felt sturdier and they had reached one of the buildings he'd seen from a distance.

The massive stairway was as wide as the building. The doors were almost as tall and Marco craned his neck to see the writing above one of them. He had only read, "The place of the cure of the soul... " when the doors swung open and a group of young men burst through, their arms full of scrolls.

"Now's our chance! Hurry!" commanded Cicero. He swiftly scooted between a tangle of legs and disappeared into the building. Marco was too busy gawking, and the doors closed with a thud. Alone on the covered portico, he wandered the wide, now empty space, feeling insignificant in the presence of such immensity.

After what seemed like forever, the door opened narrowly and a young boy squeezed through. Marco took his chance and darted into the slit, his tail caught by the closing door. He yelped as he shot into the building and almost missed Cicero, who was resting under a bench.

Marco washed his bruised tail, which did not hurt as much as his injured pride.

"Keep up with me," Cicero ordered. "If you dawdle or wander off, we may never find each other in this place."

Marco kept silent. Instead he considered the library building as he trotted along behind Cicero. Light streaming in from lofty windows on the pale blue walls gave the impression they were still outside. Clay pots and baskets invited him to investigate. Giant marble columns drew his attention upwards to a ceiling dotted with domes and skylights. A pool of clear running water called him to drink, but he didn't dare stop. Cicero was moving at a good clip.

Passing through a towering arched doorway, they entered a room full of long high tables where young men stood, busily engaged in something Marco could not see. They were not discussing the stars or navigational charts, but their intense, focused energy saturated the room.

"What is that strange sound?" he asked Cicero.

"Books were hand printed in the fourth century," Cicero said. "That is the sound of many reed pens put to papyrus—the sound of the scribes."

Young boys carried bundles of rolled papers in and out of wide interior doors. Their conversation, muted and sparse, drifted upwards. Marco yawned and thought fondly of a nap.

Suddenly a group of men burst through the doors and several young boys rushed over to receive armfuls of rolled papyrus. With practiced efficiency, the young attendants distributed them to the scribes.

Marco and Cicero had sought refuge from the hustle and bustle, observing the surge of activity from under a bench.

"A boat has come into port!" Cicero declared. "I love the harbor. We must go down there sometime. They are always plenty of fish heads for the taking."

The mention of food made Marco hungry, but he asked, "What do boats and fish heads have to do with the library?"

"Boats bring books! Merchants brought their books and scrolls with them on their long journeys. Even the new Roman codices found their way here. Alexandrians valued them even more than merchants' goods, because all scrolls and books were taken before their owners were even allowed to disembark."

As if illustrating his story, hundreds of papyrus scrolls were being rolled out in the hall.

"You see, the scribes waste no time," Cicero said. "When they are finished copying, runners return them to their owners still on the ships. I've heard rumors, though, that the original books often stay here, and their owners only got back a good copy."

Cicero scooted out from under the chair. "Come. Now I want to show you something *really* interesting."

Marco was perfectly content to stay under the chair. Why leave this beautiful dreamlike palace full of books? He began purring himself into a nap and allowed his eyes to close.

"Suit yourself," said Cicero.

Even with his eyes closed, Marco felt Cicero's absence. He opened one eye in time to see him heading towards one of the doors.

For a brief moment, he thought of the advantages of being on his own. Without this mysterious companion who seemed bent on leading him into stranger and stranger territories, he would be free to plant himself right here. As appealing as the idea was, something made him get up anyway.

Curiosity and Cicero's magic. They drew him like a magnet.

Maybe I'll just see where he's going. It can't be any stranger than time traveling.

STRANGE PASSAGE

Marco had to scurry. He almost lost him when the old cat disappeared in a tangle of legs. Marco maneuvered his way through the crowd, barely catching sight of the tip of his tail, when Cicero made yet another swift turn. Marco broke into a run, dodging library patrons and scribes.

Cicero was disappearing down a long gloomy hallway. No more spacious, sky lit rooms, or the hustle and bustle of activity. Another turn and Marco was following Cicero down a dim stairway, one that seemed to be plunging them deeper and deeper under the great main hall. With each step, the passageway grew darker. With each turn of direction, Marco felt doubt and anxiety turning his stomach.

Why was Cicero always taking him down dark stairways? Once again, he bemoaned his decision to follow this cat. He swore that, if he ever escaped, he would go home and take his adventures from books—and only from books.

Grumbling to himself, he ran headlong into Cicero. The absolute darkness of the place made it impossible to see, even with his exceptional sight. Cicero sat immobile, like a statue, but unlike a statue, warmth radiated from him.

Marco took comfort in this, in spite of everything. What on earth was Cicero waiting for? And why did they need to come to this black hole of a place when there was a perfectly lovely library upstairs?

The dense silence was suffocating. A stab of fear gripped him, and he would have bolted if only he could see where he was going. He hated total darkness. The way it closed in on him... the way it grabbed him. His throat tightened.

A sound broke his morbidity; a sound so bizarre it would have frightened him except it was so fantastic.

It was the sound of laughter.

Wisps of flickering light bounced wildly around the hard stone walls, growing brighter, but not in a gradual way. Light and laughter moved down the stairs in bits and bursts. Things could not get any stranger, thought Marco.

"It took you long enough to get here," Cicero said to the still-invisible being.

"I found some old friends." The voice reverberated out of the darkness. "It's been centuries-uries," she said in an echo-y voice.

"We have no time for visiting, Alaniah. Not this trip."

"Patience, my dear Cicero-ero-oh... We have come such a long way-ay-ay... You can wait a moment longer."

The creature emerged from the darkness and fluttered into the stairwell. Marco was certain he'd seen everything by now, but hovering above him was a shimmering creature with iridescent wings. Its voice sounded like nothing he'd ever heard, sort of singing or laughing. No, maybe it was like bells. Not the big ones, but the small silvery ones.

"I think he sees me now-ow," she lilted.

"A good sign," said Cicero. "Marco, this is Alaniah, our tour guide."

Alaniah flew around his head, inspecting him. "He's very young," she said to Cicero as though Marco couldn't hear.

"Yes, but I believe he's the one," answered Cicero.

"The last one, you believed in him as well-ell," she said.

Distracted by her beauty, Marco paid little attention to their words.

"Yes," Cicero continued. "And I wasted too much time on him. Time is not something I can squander now."

"A bit grumpy aren't we, Cicero-ero?"

"Dear Alaniah, you know I am getting on in years. Even with your gifts to me, you must remember I am a mortal creature."

Alaniah responded with a haunted sigh.

"Oh, Alaniah," breathed Cicero. "I wish not to be the cause of your sadness. Your light expanded my life, and when I have 'shuffled off this mortal coil,' as Shakespeare said, I will have no regrets."

"I do not know the meaning of regret. Explain, please."

"How can I tell you about something only mortals suffer?"

"This one. You feel he is trustworthy-orthy?"

By now Marco realized something was up, and that something was about him.

"We will discover the truth soon," said Cicero. "Now Alaniah, please let us in."

"By all means, as you are fond of saying-ing." Then Alaniah folded up within herself, not unlike a morning glory folding up for the evening, but a soft glow still shone through her translucent wrapping.

Then Alaniah burst open, transforming the dark dungeon into something almost festive, showering them with light glitter like it was the Fourth of July.

"A bit extravagant," teased Cicero. "Showing off for your admirer?"

"Just being practical, Cicero. Now we can all see."

It was true. Alaniah hovered in front of an elaborately carved doorway. The doorknocker, a heavy bronze ring, creaked and rose on its hinge as though an invisible hand lifted it. Then the ring fell.

The tiny space reverberated with an earsplitting, echoing sound like the peal of a church bell from inside the tower. The door shattered and fell at the same moment, sheets of small particles cascading into a heap on the floor.

When the dust settled, his ears were still ringing, but Marco could not believe what was on the other side of the door. Now he must surely be dreaming.

"MORE THINGS IN HEAVEN AND EARTH… "

On the other side of the door was a massive room, although 'room' was too small of a word to describe the space. As large as one of the enormous halls above ground, it was certainly not what Marco expected to find at the bottom of some dark, dank stairs. Illuminated by orbs of moving light, which Marco discovered were hundreds of creatures like Alaniah, it was hard to tell where the walls or ceiling began or ended.

Cicero breathed a deep sigh of contentment and stepped over the pile of debris that had been the door. Alaniah fluttered through, and Marco barely made it before the door began magically reassembling itself.

They descended marble stairs into a vast cavernous hall.

"Welcome! Welcome!" Approaching them eagerly was a young olive-skinned man in a green tunic, accompanied by a gray cat. "Welcome Cicero, Alaniah!" He reached down and petted Cicero lovingly. "It is always too long between visits, isn't it? I trust your journey was pleasant enough, yes?"

"It went well, yes," Cicero said.

"And who do we have here?" asked the young man, smiling down at Marco.

"Introductions, Cicero." Alaniah bubbled rather than spoke. Marco loved listening to the fairy-like creature, who seemed to take nothing seriously.

"Of course," said Cicero. He scratched his head, and Marco recognized his action as cover for his embarrassment, but Cicero quickly returned to full posture and spoke clearly. "I'd like to present to you the Keeper of *The Book of Motion*, a noble Librarian, Guardian of the Guardians, Keeper of the Sword of Knowledge—"

"Greetings, Marco," the man, interrupted, holding his hand up to stop Cicero. "Cicero gets a little carried away sometimes. My name is Akeel." He reached down and scratched Marco's head and neck. "Welcome to our Library."

"You have a new addition, Akeel," said Cicero, nodding at a spiral stairway. The stairs were transparent and reflected the colors of the room. They were also not attached to each other—or anything else, for that matter.

"This is our latest addition. I am most excited about it. Come. I will show you," Akeel said, walking towards the far corner where the stairs began. "They were designed by one of our brightest new mathematicians. It is based on the Golden Spiral, and the invisible support structure is established on principles that would take months to explain. We have been studying Sacred Geometry, and this project was the result of our studies."

The crystal blocks formed a wide, sweeping curve from the floor. As they rose higher, they turned inwards on themselves in a small circle. Two people stood halfway up the ramp; one, a young boy and the other, an older bearded man. Marco reached out to touch the luminous step.

"They're made of crystal," Akeel said in a voice close to reverent. "Magnificent, isn't it?"

Marco, who couldn't contain his curiosity, began climbing the steps, but Akeel called him back.

Marco reluctantly obeyed, but he kept looking upwards to see where the stairs ended.

"You are observant Marco, but there's a reason you cannot see where it goes," Akeel said. "The Golden Spiral stairs have no end. They continue into infinity. When a climber reaches a certain point... well... they pass into another dimension, but that's a trip for another time."

Marco felt light headed just thinking about what Akeel said.

"Come. There are many things to see in the inner Library, and I would love to give you a tour."

Akeel led them down a hallway of towering doorways and Marco imagined the closed doors hid wonderful secrets. Through one of the opened doors, Marco observed men and women moving in slow, dance-like motions. Through another, he saw bearded men on low cushions, reading or dozing. Several rooms were full of children busily engaged in reading or playing. Marco had to run to catch up with Akeel and Cicero.

Akeel talked as they walked. "Above ground are the treasures of the world, the great discoveries and inventions made by humans. They are looked after by, how do I say... by our more conventional Guardian Librarians."

"Here below is the Library within the Library, which holds treasures from a higher realm. Books holding knowledge from beyond this world. The humans you see here are in training to be Guardians of these Sacred Texts."

"They must go through rigorous training before they are accepted as defenders of these treasures," Akeel said. "Hey, Chuluum, there you are." Akeel reached down to pick up the gray cat Marco had seen when they first arrived.

Chuluum smugly examined Marco and Cicero from his elevated position in Akeel's arms. He began to hiss, but Akeel was too quick.

"Be nice, Chuluum. They are my friends," Akeel said, chuckling at his petulant cat.

Akeel motioned for Marco and Cicero to follow and led the way into a room full of books and dozing cats. But they passed through until they reached yet another door. Marco had never seen so many doors in one place.

"Do you think he's ready?" Akeel asked Cicero.

"I suppose it's time to find out," Cicero answered.

Akeel dropped Chuluum out of his arms and opened the door to reveal what looked like a large closet. Alaniah entered first, casting light in the small space, empty except for a single table.

Akeel waited until they were all in and approached the table. Marco hadn't noticed the wooden box until Akeel leaned over and blew on it. The box disappeared, dissolving into a cloud of fairy-like dust, which settled into piles. The disappearance of the magical box exposed a fairly ordinary book. Akeel blew more dust off as he picked it up.

Cicero was on the table, nuzzling and purring against Akeel's arm.

"This is the reason we came," Cicero said. "You needed to see the book in its original time and place."

Skeptical but curious, Marco jumped up to join the others. There was nothing special about the book that he could see, but Alaniah was creating a distraction by flitting back and forth like a hummingbird.

"Alaniah, please hold still," Akeel requested.

They waited until she calmed down, hovering above them in more or less the same spot.

"*The Book of Motion!*" Cicero announced to Marco in a grand manner, as if he were announcing the arrival of a noble prince.

Marco was perplexed. He knew he was supposed to be impressed, but it was a long way to come for a book. What was the big deal about motion? Waking from a nap and walking to the food bowl or stalking a mouse. That was motion.

Then Marco wondered if his eyes were playing tricks on him. The book seemed to quiver and sort of exhale like some kind of living, breathing thing.

Okay, maybe not such an ordinary book, Marco thought.

Cicero tried to explain. "Motion can be as simple as getting from point A to point B, but it can have far deeper implications. The modest title is a bit misleading, but I think it's to protect the importance of what's inside."

"You are right, Cicero," said Akeel. "We are talking about

motion on an entirely different level—the subatomic scale, which no one can see, even with special instruments…"

"Speak for yourselves, poor earthlings," Alaniah interrupted.

Akeel glanced up and smiled, but didn't miss a beat. "…where things move very fast. Did you know the velocity of electrons can reach up to two million meters per second?"

"Um…"

"Even faster," Cicero added. "Some travel three hundred million meters per second… the speed of light."

Marco cocked his head, trying hard to look like he understood.

"Of course, this will not become common knowledge until your time."

"Of course," replied Marco, feeling it to be a safe response.

"In your time," continued Akeel, "scientists will begin to grasp some of the ideas in this book. That door will open for them, but unfortunately, some will lack good judgment in using it—being responsible with its power."

Akeel paused, looking a bit distressed. "And they will have learned nothing without this insight. Even quantum physics, quarks and all, cannot explain the whole picture. Only this small book, *The Book of Motion*, holds the key to understanding the grand scheme of things."

Marco sighed, suddenly overcome by a wave of homesickness, wherever home was.

"I'm sure you wonder why I have brought you here," said Cicero. "And while you might not understand, you will have to trust me—trust us."

If that was supposed to soothe him, it didn't help, because Marco thought it highly unfair. A sudden itch begged to be scratched and he took his time in order to gather his senses.

Cicero and Akeel paid no attention, absorbed in their discussion. They seemed to be sharing threads of the conversation as though they possessed the same mind.

"Everything is in constant motion," Cicero was saying. "Electrons whirl like dervishes around their nucleus, planets whirl around their sun and stars whirl within their galaxies. This book is simply the ultimate guidebook to understanding everything in its natural state of motion."

Marco had no idea what an electron, a nucleus, or a dervish was, but he did know something about the stars.

Akeel set the book back on the table. "No one knows its true origin, but it appears to have come from some other world. *The Book of Motion* is the most amazing book in the library; unlike most scientific explanations of life, this one leaves room for God. No, that does not do it justice." He tried again. "*The Book of Motion* is more like an affirmation, as though sent by a Higher Power to show us what is possible."

Akeel rubbed his hands over his face. "I'm afraid I am not explaining this well and I know the Book better than anyone."

"You are troubled Akeel, and not just about explanations."

"Yes," he replied as he began pacing the room. "It's about the reports I've been getting. There have been burnings and lootings in distant village libraries. A new force seeking to gain power is creating disturbances, spreading rumors about us, about the Library. I fear that they would like nothing better than to see us buried for good."

Akeel sighed. "The Guardians have already been driven underground in order to protect these treasured books." He looked out through the open door towards the other rooms full of books. "But what will become of all those who openly thirst for knowledge, both worldly and divine? This small but ill-intentioned group sees everything as black and white and they are forcing their views on others. They even perceive God in this limited perspective, as if He were some trifling old man who exhausted himself creating the universe and has been taking a long nap ever since."

Akeel was clearly agitated. "They spread black clouds over people's minds so they can carry out their dishonorable deeds and seize power under the cover of darkness. Even worse, they believe they can blot out our memory of the mysterious, our divine origin! How is it possible that others believe these pitiful notions? But their influence is growing, and I fear this grand idea which has become the Library of Alexandria has reached its zenith."

A deep sigh escaped from Cicero and resonated like a wave through the room. Marco could not help joining the sigh. Cicero moved to Akeel's side and nuzzled his head against him. This was a softer aspect of Cicero that Marco had not seen. At home, the old cat rarely interacted with the librarians, preferring to keep to himself and his books.

"Yes, I see why it needs to be guarded," Marco said, thinking he was starting to understand and wanting very much to contribute to the conversation.

"But you don't," said Cicero, a little harshly. "Not yet, anyway." The old cat jumped down and began pacing in step behind Akeel. "There is something worse that can happen to it..." Cicero glanced up at Akeel's back. "The very people who want to suppress knowledge are the ones who know how powerful it is. They foolishly believe it is something they can own. Something they can hoard away like gold."

Marco sighed quietly. He sat alone on the table watching man and cat pace in sync around the small room.

"I do not know yet whether they seek to destroy us or dominate us, but if they ever acquired *The Book of Motion*..." Akeel dropped his head into his hands.

"What?" Marco couldn't help asking, even though he figured it was a dumb question.

"Marco, the most important thing you need to know is that *The Book of Motion* was a gift..." He paused. "Bestowed upon humankind for our understanding and benefit. But like anything, it can be used according to the intentions of its keeper. Take a carpenter's ax for instance. It can be used to fell trees and create, to build dwellings for families. Or it can bludgeon the life out of someone."

Alaniah darted about the small room. "Cicero! Akeel!" she sputtered, showering them with microscopic light crystals.

"Yes, Alaniah? What is the matter?"

"Get on with it!"

"What do you mean?" Both Akeel and Cicero looked perplexed.

"Too much talking-ing."

Cicero and Akeel looked at each other, then at Marco. Brilliant minds suddenly clueless.

"Oh, mortal beings, you are so dense." Alaniah whirled in front of them. "You must show him the Book! Isn't that why you brought him here-re?"

"You are right, Alaniah," said Akeel. "We have been caught up in our own thoughts. Poor Marco." Marco welcomed Akeel's quick caress and stretched out for more. Instead Akeel stepped over to the book, leaving Marco lying on his back.

He scrambled to get up as Akeel said, "You have traveled far, my young friend. I will make it worth your effort."

Akeel collected himself by closing his eyes, taking a deep breath and clearing his throat. He spoke in a language Marco didn't understand, and with both hands, gently opened the book.

A magnitude of light came bursting from inside the book, like water liberated through the turn of a spigot. It filled the room, transforming the walls into a kaleidoscope of radiance. Constellations, algebraic formulas, and whirling dervishes swirled together. Marco grew dizzy watching the wall of revolving images, vaguely reminiscent of his time travel experience. Many of them were little more than a blur, except for a few strange ones—wild horses racing across desert sand and a young monk in a bare candlelit room, writing at a small desk.

How did all this come from inside the book?

Marco went over to look at the open pages of strange script. He thought he'd seen a lot of books, but never anything like this. The pages were made of some material that reminded him of the crystalline spiral staircase, only paper thin. It appeared to be alive.

Gradually the marvelous show subsided and the room returned to normal. But nothing was really what Marco would call normal anymore.

"I will now give you a simple demonstration of its power," said Akeel, pulling out a knife hidden in the folds of his tunic. In one smooth movement, he sliced his hand. Bright red blood seeped from the cut.

THE RIGHT FREQUENCY

Akeel held his right hand over the book as blood pooled in his other hand. Marco thought Cicero should be more worried, but he acted like he'd seen this before. Akeel moved his right hand in a circle above the wound. The blood and the cut both disappeared, as though it had never happened.

Marco was speechless.

Akeel smiled. "This was merely a parlor trick… to show you its healing power. But you asked why it needs guarding. That requires something a little more novel." He assured Cicero, "We will keep it simple and not *too* showy."

Akeel picked up Chuluum and placed him on the table. The cat tried to bolt, but Akeel was quick. With a few words and a wave of his arm, Akeel transformed Chuluum into a small squirming gray ball.

Marco could hardly believe his eyes. Chuluum was gone and a mouse had taken his place.

Alaniah flew in jittery circles above their heads. The mouse jumped out of Akeel's grasp and Cicero pounced on him. The squirming cat-turned-mouse went limp and Marco feared he was dead.

"Here, let me have him," Akeel said. "I don't want him scratching you when I change him back."

Akeel cupped the mouse in his hands and blew gently. Suddenly Chuluum became his old self and tumbled to the floor. His fur ruffled and his whiskers twitched with humiliation, but he puffed out his chest and glared at Marco like it was his fault. Then he high-tailed it out of the room.

"Poor Chuluum," said Marco. Five minutes ago he thought the cat was arrogant and annoying. Now he was a little sorry for him. "Will he be alright?"

"He's fine. He won't come out of hiding for a while, but he'll forgive me. He knows I mean him no harm. But you can see why the Book's power is not to be played with. I needed a quick way to show you what some people call magic and others call God—and why they will go to extreme measures to try and possess it."

Alaniah had calmed and was floating above. Strains of music drifted in from a distance, or maybe it was coming from her. Marco couldn't tell.

"Few cats are able to hear the music," Cicero said.

The sound grew more intense until it reverberated throughout his body. Like a magnanimous purr or the roaring of Niagara Falls. Or the singing of angels.

"How come I can hear it?" Marco asked Cicero.

"You have to be tuned to the right channel. Most cats don't operate on that frequency."

"It's a good sign. You've done well picking this one," Akeel told Cicero.

"I'm thinking he picked me."

"Could be," said Akeel. "More likely, it is the hand of destiny."

Akeel went over and stroked Marco on his head. "We will put the book away for now. It's time to tell you more of the story."

Marco burrowed into Akeel's hand and Akeel picked him up, embracing him as he closed the Book. He blew on the dust particles and they rematerialized to their former state as a box.

"Let us go elsewhere, where we can make ourselves comfortable." Akeel led them out of the small chamber into a room plump with books. Delightfully disordered, shelves were bursting with books which overflowed onto low tables and sitting cushions.

People who were reading or talking paid them no mind as Akeel cleared a space on a low cushioned platform and settled cross-legged on the divan. Chuluum, still ruffled, glared at them from his hiding place between piles of books across the room.

When they were comfortable, Akeel turned to Marco. "You have a lot of questions, no?"

"No? Oh, but yes," said Marco. "I don't even know where to start, except I have one for Cicero. Why did you bring me here? I mean, why *me*?"

"That will become obvious," Cicero answered. "But not yet. There is more to learn and..." Cicero's eyes pierced his soul. "You must be found worthy."

Marco shuddered and the conversation died. After a moment Akeel spoke. "You see all these men and women around you? They may look like casual readers enjoying a

THE RIGHT FREQUENCY

pleasant afternoon in this small library room. But do not let appearances deceive you. They are warriors of the highest order, Guardians of knowledge."

They didn't look like warriors to Marco. He'd read plenty of adventure books and none of the heroes sat around reading.

"They must pass many trials before they arrive here. Many do not make it for various reasons, but even if they pass all the others, the problem comes with the test of power."

While Akeel explained, Cicero got up, stretched and began to pace.

Akeel talked as if remembering. "In the beginning, the taste of power is sweet, savored on the tongue, like fine wine. It whispers promises in your ear and pretends to be your friend. It is easy to become addicted to this feeling.

"If you do not resist the lure of power, you become hooked. Then you begin to gather small crimes, in layers, like thin cloth, one covering another. Insignificant things, they must seem at first. A little dishonesty. Perhaps the implication of an innocent person in some misdeed. Lies, pretense and betrayals wrap themselves like a cloak and the imposter becomes nothing more than an actor in his own play."

His brow furrowed. "If it were only that uncomplicated. Everything we do affects the molecules around us. Just being here changes things in ways we cannot see." Then he made a strange statement. "But when duplicity is disguised behind a mask of honor, the consequences ripple like waves throughout time."

Cicero stopped pacing. "I have been trying to remember something I read, a quote by a famous man."

Akeel's strained face relaxed. "You are always full of good quotes, Cicero."

"It was spoken by a man named Abraham Lincoln. He said, 'Nearly all men can stand adversity, but if you want to test a man's character, give him power.' I always liked that one."

"A wise observation," said Akeel. "He must have been an honorable man. Maybe a Guardian as well." He paused, reflecting further. "A man with power will show his true character. Eventually. But many spend all their time making themselves more clever, concealing their intentions.

"I have met with this kind of deception, Akeel," Cicero said sadly. "I fear that I have not been a wisest of Guardians."

"Do not blame yourself, Cicero. We have all had encounters with betrayal and treachery."

Marco had a question forming in him that seemed to have nothing to do with Akeel's speech. Nothing and yet, everything. Only a short time ago, he longed to regain his former life. Now he felt an even stronger attraction to being here, to the Library and Akeel. In fact, he never wanted to leave. "Would it be possible for me… to stay?" Marco blurted out.

"Dear Marco," said Cicero in a rare moment of grandfatherly affection. "Be careful what you ask for." Cicero then climbed into Akeel's lap. "But I know exactly how you feel. I would stay forever too, if it were my choice."

Akeel looked at him curiously. "Hey Cicero, I have never known you to be so affectionate." He stroked Cicero's head, and they sat together for a moment.

Suddenly Chuluum darted out, aiming straight for Akeel. Cicero sorrowfully, but graciously surrendered his spot to its rightful owner. Marco had a newfound respect for both cats.

"Cicero?" Marco asked, realizing that the humans in the room had never given them a glance. "I think that nobody else knows we are here. Only Akeel and Chuluum."

Cicero answered with nothing more than a cryptic smile. At that moment, Alaniah flew over to join them.

"Enjoying your visit, Alaniah?" Cicero asked.

She answered by flying in wide, ecstatic loops over their heads. Trails of colored crystalline sifted downwards and Alaniah disappeared amongst the others.

"What *is* she?" Marco asked, after licking the fine dust that glowed momentarily on his coat.

"Alaniah is a creature of stardust," Akeel answered. "She's a Losring."

Marco tried spotting her in the swirling radiance high above them, then she was suddenly right in front of his face, like a glowing butterfly.

To Cicero she said, "Shouldn't we show him coming events?"

The spiral staircase

"I'm not ready," Cicero answered heavily. "Because I know what's coming,"

Alaniah hovered over her earthly charges. "He must see for himself," she insisted gently.

Cicero sighed. "For that we need to take another trip." He closed his eyes.

"Dear Cicero," said Alaniah. "We will try a new means of travel, very easy. Follow me." She raced off. Marco and Cicero both hung back, not ready to leave their friends. Akeel bid them farewell and Chuluum, who had recovered his dignity, came over and 'nosed' Marco goodbye.

Alaniah led the two cats into the grand hall, where they had first arrived. The room glittered and she glided among the others, as if they were all exotic sea creatures.

"Okay, Cicero," she said, startling him as she landed on his head. "Are you ready?"

Cicero wiped his paw over his eyes, as if brushing off worrisome thoughts. "Show me this new method of traveling."

"We will use the Golden Spiral." They had arrived at the foot of the staircase and turned to look at the transparent floating steps winding from the floor in an enormous curve upwards to ever-narrowing circles.

"Most unusual, Alaniah," Cicero said. "I have seen spiral staircases, but none like this. Why is it so oddly shaped?"

"Odd? I think it's beautiful-iful."

"I'm wondering why they are so wide at the bottom and so narrow at the top?"

"Oh earthling, this is a transition spiral, used for mortals. Mostly human, not cats. But then, you are not a normal cat, are you?" Alaniah whirled. "Are you trying to delay this journey, Cicero?"

"No. No. We'll be on with it, but I am curious about the staircase."

"Like Akeel explained, it is a means to let humans experience what they are too dense to see. It's also a doorway from your limited earthly world to... well, to other worlds."

With that, Alaniah twirled upwards, disappearing in what would normally be a ceiling, but nothing was quite what it appeared to be in this library. Then she spiraled downwards and came to face them, hovering in her rippling nature.

"Come, follow me."

They followed Alaniah up the floating staircase, rising and turning with each step, making Marco light headed, especially when he made the mistake of looking down.

"Keep your head up, Marco," counseled Alaniah. "Mortals who climb the Golden Spiral get… what do they call it? 'Dizzy,' I think. What a funny word."

Marco grew dizzier as they approached ever-smaller circles of the higher spheres. Cicero kept close to his side and Marco wondered how he, who loved the highest branches of the trees, even when the wind swung him to and fro, could be having difficulty climbing these simple steps.

"This is as far as we can go. Even cats are not advanced enough to travel higher. Please sit and observe," Alaniah commanded. She raised one graceful wing and pulled back something like a gauzy veil, which had been invisible until then. She held it open so they could enter.

Then Alaniah flew through, and the veil closed behind them.

PARADISE LOST

Alaniah took Marco and Cicero forward through time in their journey into the past It was a unique placement, between past and future, but not in the present, and only beings like Alaniah could successfully navigate this realm.

"Now we will see what became of the great grand idea called the Library of Alexandria."

They were in a vast arena covered by a dome the color of a pre-dawn sky. After a small flicker of light, the dome filled with images, all spinning around him, making him slightly dizzy. Gradually they slowed until the same room where they had left Akeel and Chuluum came into view, but Marco hardly recognized it. People who had been quietly reading were now sweeping books and scrolls off the shelves, stuffing them into bags.

The library, which had been a place of calm, was filled with chaos and confusion. Alexandria, where earth-shattering ideas were born out of the very atmosphere which people breathed, had been attacked. Even viewed through the filter of this cosmic display, Marco smelled panic and knew he was witnessing the birth of tragedy. Paradise had been invaded.

Akeel was there, in the middle, like a well-anchored tree in the midst of a storm. He urged them to take as many books as possible.

Marco flinched when the banging began, angry pounding from somewhere he couldn't see. Akeel shouted, "The tunnel! Go! Now!" He was shepherding everyone towards the back. "Leave the rest!"

The men and women, toting leather bags heavy with books, stumbled over each other in the mad rush to escape the assault of invaders.

The main door, battered by brute force, splintered open. Shouts of the soldiers were harsh and quick, like knife jabs. There were perhaps a dozen of them, their faces hidden behind metal helmets with black holes in the headgear where their eyes should have been. Marco shivered at the sight of them.

Akeel, after ushering the last of the guardians out, grabbed his bag and Chuluum. But the helmeted men were at his back, and the foremost soldier drew his dagger. Akeel swung around, dropping the bag and cat in one smooth motion. He moved through the hooded men as though his body was his weapon, with fluid movements that resembled a dance more than a fight.

One after another his attackers fell. Metal clanged as soft-bodied men in their exoskeletons of armor collided with each other. Akeel had no armor that Marco could see, but his defense appeared effortless, as though he had some invisible shield around him.

When the turbulence died, Akeel opened the tunnel door to join the exodus of librarians. He did not see the lone black figure creep out from the shadows, dagger aimed at his back. Marco jumped up, certain that Akeel was about to be killed, and here he was, helpless to do anything. Again. He didn't want to watch, but he couldn't keep from it either. The man's blade plunged. Marco cringed.

In the microsecond before the knife pierced Akeel's back, a shower of crystalline light exploded in the face of the assassin and his hand missed its mark. A cluster of Losrings had intervened. They aimed their blinding light on the killer, relentlessly driving him backwards until he turned and ran.

The screen went black, plunging them into darkness. Marco was practically beside himself, wondering what had happened, when the screen appeared again. Now Akeel and the others were crawling through a crude tunnel, heaving their bags in front of them, struggling on hands and knees with their cumbersome loads.

There was light at the end of the tunnel, but it did not come from the sun. Marco's view of what awaited them outside was blocked by the scuffle of librarians pulling themselves and their bags out of the tunnel, silhouetted against a bright orange blaze behind them.

A clear view showed not one but many huge fires lighting up the Library's concourse. A dozen or so bonfires burned in perfectly straight lines, as if they had been planted in an orchard. Black butterflies skipped through the air above the fires, people were celebrating, and Marco thought it was a frightening but glorious sight.

Akeel called to the others to follow him as he ran behind a small building and ordered everyone to stay. He moved towards the fires, keeping low to the ground. Marco had never seen a human look like he was stalking prey. Then the light from the flames revealed a look of horror on Akeel's face.

Cicero would not speak, so Alaniah tried to explain. She told him that the soldiers had drained the water and filled the fountains to the brim with books, poured oil over them and lit them with torches.

Alaniah's account of what was happening made him angry at her for suggesting such a dreadful idea.

"You're lying!" he shouted at her. Alaniah's crisp retort was in some language he didn't understand. Marco sat for a moment, trying to absorb the impossible concept.

"But..." He hardly knew what to say. "Books? Why would they want to burn books?"

"I do not understand the ways of humans," was her bleak response. After that, Marco sat in silence with Cicero hunched next to him. He had to remind himself that what was happening was real because it seemed more like a bad dream.

In a carnival-like atmosphere, women sat eating, while their children played at the perimeter of the fire's light. Books and scrolls were piled in heaps like burial mounds around the fires. Men joked and laughed as they threw the books in.

Marco heard a man say, "Fire is such a beautiful thing." It was at that moment he realized those weren't black butterflies he'd seen—they were fragments of scorched paper.

"Brilliant, I'd say!" said another man.

"This'll teach those big heads a thing or two."

"Librarians," said another, spitting on the ground.

"Intell-ect-u-als. Think they're so smart. So high and mighty."

The reflection of fire on the men's creased faces made them even more hideous.

"Common thieves, that's what they are. These books are all stolen you know!"

"Jail would be too good for these criminals!"

One man tilted his head back and took a swig from his flask, then poured the rest of its contents on the fire. "You need this more than me," he said to the fire, which responded with a flourish of deep orange. There were shouts of approval.

A man pushed forward through the crowd. "Stop! This is crazy! Think of the children! How will they learn about history? About the heavens?"

Somebody grabbed the protestor and shoved him to the ground. "Who do you think we're doing this for? This *is* about our children!"

The dissenter tried to get up, but another man pinned him to the ground with his boot. "These books are brainwashing our children."

"Yeah," agreed one of the arsonists. "Our kids think they're smarter than us. My son, he's twelve and he thinks he's too smart to work in the fields. Too smart for his own good, I tell him. But I know how to knock sense into him."

The dissenter moaned as one of the fire men, as Marco thought of them, kicked him in the groin.

"We knew it was time for action when we caught our kids sneaking off to the library. These new-fangled ideas are dangerous."

Someone in the back of the crowd shouted, 'Save the children!' and the others took it up like a battle cry. The ones closest to the fire, reinvigorated, lobbed armfuls of books on the blaze.

Barbarians at the Gate

Akeel crept backwards, making no sound even as he stumbled over Chuluum, who suddenly appeared at his side. He headed back to where he'd left the others, but they were gone.

Akeel heaved his bag over his shoulder, picked up Chuluum and turned from the burning landscape out towards the darkness, hiking through wild scrub and rocks under a moonless sky. He did not stop until he reached a massive stone wall far from the main city.

Akeel put the cat on the ground. "I can't climb the wall with both you and the bag. You're on your own." He started climbing.

When Akeel reached the top of the wall, he stopped and turned. Chuluum was still on the ground, a silent meow pleading for help, but Akeel scolded him instead.

"Chuluum! This wall is no great challenge for you." Akeel sighed. "Don't you understand? I am sick at heart. Look behind you. Hundreds of years of collecting destroyed in one night." Akeel dropped his head. "I didn't think they would take it this far."

Akeel lowered the heavy leather bag where it was within the cat's reach, but Chuluum just sniffed at it.

"Chuluum! You are being one difficult cat. Come! We must go find the others." This time Chuluum grabbed hold and Akeel lifted him to the top of the wall.

Hoisting the bag over his shoulder and tucking his cat inelegantly under one arm, Akeel leaped. He landed on both feet.

The boundary wall of the city, which afforded relative safety, was behind them. They were now in territory that belonged exclusively to thieves and barbarians. Chuluum immediately ran off into the darkness.

Akeel moved toward a shapeless form on the ground.

"Sirus!" He cried out, dropping down next to his friend, whose head was soaked in blood.

"You missed all the fun," Sirus said hoarsely.

"Barbarians at the gates! Why didn't I see this coming?" Akeel wiped some of the blood from around his friend's eyes.

"Don't blame yourself," Sirus said. "Who could imagine such brutality? We lived in a dream world, I think."

"We have been awakened by mad men," Akeel said. "They've stolen our life, our books... our dreams."

"Not as long as you carry some of them with you." Sirus closed his eyes and struggled to speak. "Don't give up. Escape now." His voice faded to a whisper. "I just don't know how you'll manage without me."

Akeel shook his head. "Don't worry. I'm going to get you out of here." He looked out at the desolate landscape that merged into nothingness, a black void.

Sirus stopped breathing. Akeel shook him. "Don't, Sirus! We're companions. We always travel together, don't we?"

Sirus recovered a breath, but Akeel barely understood him now. He was only able to make out, "...a different kind of journey."

"You traveled just last month. No more days off." Akeel tried to laugh. He thought as long as they could share a joke, his best friend might recover and he would not lose him along with everything else.

Sirus was still struggling for each breath, but he seemed to revive enough to rekindle Akeel's hopes. The dying man grabbed his hand with a surprisingly firm grip and said, "I think you're going to actually miss me."

Sirus reached inside his tunic and handed a book to Akeel. "Leave this graveyard or your fate will be the same as mine."

Akeel squeezed Sirus's hand and stared into his face, as though his will would keep him alive.

Sirus's next breath never came.

A pale sky-blue mist seemed to radiate from his body. For a brief moment, it pulsed like a heartbeat, then dispersed and drifted upwards, merging with a milky white light.

The clipped sound of voices from a distance broke through the fleeting moment of grace. The barbarians were getting closer. He closed his companion's vacant eyes. Sirus' body, unoccupied by his spirit, appeared as spent as an extinguished campfire. He pressed Sirus' book into his bag. There was no time for mourning, but Akeel couldn't leave him lying out in the open. He began to drag his friend towards the dubious shelter of the fortress wall. On the way he stumbled over another body. Akeel released hold on his friend and stood straight to survey the dark terrain. Now he saw that what had looked like scrub brush under the moonless sky was actually dead bodies.

Enemy voices punctuating the darkness reminded him of his fate if he lingered. He would be forced to leave his friends without a traditional burial or even the simplest tribute.

A waning gibbous moon was rising, making the landscape more surreal, like the empty space between his past and future.

He had to move quickly, he knew, but his feet seemed rooted to the ground. He was now a fugitive in no-man's land, severed from home and friends. Even his cat was gone.

As if on cue, a line of silhouettes emerged from behind a desert scrub—shapes that moved like cats. They wandered through the landscape of corpses, touching each with a gentle nudge. They grew closer, and it became clear that Chuluum was leading the other cats on their sorrowful homage, giving the fallen librarians the honor they deserved.

A flame sprouted up not five hundred feet away. Triumphant voices congratulated themselves. Akeel did not have the luxury of time or sorrow. The best tribute he could pay would be to save the book each of his companions had hidden under his tunic.

With the troupe of cats following him, Akeel trekked across the barren land until they reached the river. He viewed the wide expanse of water and tightened the closures on his bag.

Then he stepped into the cold current and spoke to the cats. "If you want to survive, you'll have to get wet now."

Reluctantly the cats climbed onto the bag. Chuluum clung to his shoulder and the whole crew slipped quietly into the freezing water.

FOREVER CHANGED

Marco remembered to keep his eyes closed on the trip back, but he was forever a changed cat.

They returned to the small cave-like room under the Angel Springs Library, facing each other as though they had never left.

Cicero opened his eyes. "It's good to be home again! That was a bit easier, wasn't it?"

"Some," said Marco, grumpy. The transition back to present time had been easier, but other things bothered him.

"Yes," said Cicero. "I always found traveling forward through time rather pleasant."

Marco only half listened as Cicero and Alaniah discussed the finer elements of time travel—surfing on light waves, the directional flow of energy, portals and wormholes. He was angry at the nonchalant way they were behaving. Marco's safe world of off-the-shelf adventure books was over.

"How can you act as if nothing happened?" he demanded. Still caught between worlds, Marco asked, "Where's Akeel? Where'd he go?"

"Ah, that was many years past. Centuries ago. Although in reality, there is no time..." Cicero said, licking his paw, which always indicated he was about to plunge into one of his esoteric lectures.

"Tell me what happened to him," Marco demanded, before Cicero could start his monologue.

"Oh, he made it out. Not without plenty of difficulty, but he made it."

"And the cats?"

"Yes, the cats as well."

"And the library? And the books? All those books..." Marco trailed off. He was afraid he already knew the answer.

"Very few of the books were rescued. We don't know how many exactly, but Akeel saved *The Book of Motion* and the other sacred texts his companions had hidden inside their tunics."

"They burned," he gulped, "... all the rest?"

Cicero's silence was enough.

"But who would want to destroy a lot of harmless books?"

"Ahhh, now it is time to explore the deeper meaning of things," said Cicero.

"Why? What do you mean?"

"Why do you think books are harmless?" challenged Cicero. "Books are *not* harmless! Books are full of ideas! And ideas are powerful things."

Marco sat up straighter, straining to follow Cicero's explanation. "Watch people when they come in the library. They read and think. They leave and they do things with the ideas they've read about. You see, a human's world is very different than ours, Marco. They are complicated." He paused. "And so mysterious."

"Yes," said Marco. That was one thing they could agree on.

"I have seen the look in their eyes when their minds open, like they are being released from prison."

Marco thought pleasantly of the new worlds he'd traveled through books.

"I am not talking about fiction here!" pronounced Cicero, as if he'd read his mind.

"Ideas begin their life as small seeds, so light they may drift through the air like dust motes. If a human is fortunate enough to catch one, when the light is right, it can be planted, just like a seed. With fertile soil, it may grow into a flower or tree, which will re-seed, thus producing a whole field or forest."

Marco wasn't sure what Cicero was talking about. How did an idea become a field of flowers? He was beginning to think humans were simpler than this strange old cat, and he'd never thought humans were simple before.

Cicero kept on. "Humans have invented wonderful things from the smallest germ of an idea. Like Gutenberg's printing press. Without him, we would have no books. Then came the telescope. That's when humans could see things cats have always been able to see—stars and the outer realms of space. And how about the light bulb?" Cicero interrupted himself. "Did you know people can't see in the dark?"

"No," answered Marco, surprised. He'd always thought lamps and such were decoration.

"Let's take Isaac Newton. Sir Isaac, they called him. He was a most fantastic human. He thought about ideas all the time. He thought about motion and gravity and light and discovered more about them than anyone else in his time. And he generously shared his ideas with the world," said Cicero. "But he also gave them a warning."

"A warning?"

"More like advice to scientists. He cautioned them against using scientific laws to view the universe as a mere machine, as matter only."

Did Cicero really think he understood all this? Cicero, who was forever pulling him off into strange new worlds. Marco sighed and turned his attention to Alaniah. She was sleeping on the top of the wooden chest, looking as though she were covered with a translucent cloak, her luminous colors pulsing inside like a beating heart. Marco always felt better just looking at her.

But this stuff Cicero was talking about—he was off in a world even more remote than Alaniah's.

"Cicero, why are you telling me this? What does it have to do with the Library? I still don't know why you took me there, and now you're talking about ideas and seeds and warnings." Marco began pacing.

Cicero stopped his own pacing and studied Marco. "Forgive me. It is a shortcoming of mine. I tend to get carried away by ideas myself. You see how a perfectly good idea can become unmanageable. Ideas are anything but harmless."

"I never thought of an idea as being dangerous."

"That's because you are a pure soul. You intend no harm to anyone." Cicero's eyes followed Marco as he took to pacing.

"But how can an idea be dangerous?"

"It is the other side of the coin, so to speak."

"Coin?" Marco asked, looking up at Cicero in wonderment. He wasn't even quite sure what a coin was. He felt lost—in some ways more lost than when he was homeless or even time traveling.

"Forgive me, for I must spoil your innocence." Cicero took a moment to wash his face. "Ideas are risky. Think of it!" He commanded. "How do you know where they will lead you?" Cicero looked pointedly at Marco, who could not turn away from his gaze.

"An idea by itself is impartial. Whoever nurtures an idea, however, becomes its caretaker. If it is a person of good will, the idea will flower into something beneficial, making life better, easier, happier for many others.

"But if there are ill intentions in the mind of its master, the idea will be contaminated by that. A dark creature with powerful knowledge keeps their ideas... almost as though they were a prized pet. They feed it rich food and watch it grow. Without taming... without considering its effect on the rest of the world, they allow it to grow into a monster."

The steady light glowing within the sleeping Losring flickered, like interrupted current.

Cicero continued. "This wild beast of an idea gone bad waits, pacing like a caged animal, waiting for its time, then demanding to be unleashed."

Cicero's tail quivered and Alaniah leaped upwards like a startled butterfly, her light scattering around the cave-like walls of the room.

"Once freed, the wild beast joins forces with its caretaker, but now it has become the master. The person whose idea it was in the beginning is now under its spell and will become its slave." Cicero stared hard at Marco, as though he were hiding one of these monsters somewhere. "It is a terrible thing to cross paths with a dark force let loose."

Marco stopped breathing.

"Powerful ideas are best cared for by people not interested in using them for their own benefit. A rare combination." Cicero walked in a wide circle around Marco, examining him. "True guardians are rare. Human or cat."

"Is this what happened? I mean, at the library. Somebody got an idea that they should burn the library and all of the books?"

"Yes."

"How did they come by that idea? Where did it come from?"

"To explain that, I will have to tell you the story of the Arsonists," said Cicero.

Marco knew he was in for a long story, but he hoped he might finally get some of the answers he was looking for.

"The Arsonists were a small, but well-organized group who wanted power over the people of Alexandria," Cicero explained. "One of their main tactics was trying to control what people read. But they were clever and did not make their plans obvious. Instead, they used propaganda to persuade people that books were dangerous. Ah, Marco," Cicero said. "I am stiff from sitting. Besides, we could both use a bite to eat. I will finish the story on our way up."

Marco's tummy growled in response. They left the underground chamber and began to climb the rock stairway. Cicero continued, "Where was I? I just started to tell you about the Arsonists. Of course, they didn't call themselves that. That's my name for them. When they converted enough people to their way of thinking, they used them to do their dirty work. To their followers, they handed out titles and slogans and called them things like the 'New Reformists', anything to make them feel their actions were good and noble. Then it was easy convincing them a thorough cleansing was the only way to rid their land of dangerous books and their gate keepers, the librarians."

Marco was listening, but he also noticed that the rock passageway appeared changed. Maybe it was him that changed. When he had descended these stairs way back—how long ago it seemed—he had been full of trepidation about passing through the portal.

"When the time was right, the New Reformists, who believed the idea was theirs all along, stormed the Library, taking it under siege. They bound and gagged the librarians, scribes and patrons and dragged them off to prisons… the ones they hadn't already killed. They drained the fountains of water and filled them with books, fueled them with oil and their narrow-minded passions. The burning went on for days and weeks before all the books were consumed.

"As soon as Akeel realized what was happening, he knew the only chance to save the few books he had was to hide them. All the other Librarians had been killed, so he traveled until he found safe places, a different one for each book. But he could not stay and he would not leave them unguarded. So, everywhere he hid a book, he appointed one of the survivors."

They had almost reached the top of the stairs. "Now where's Alaniah? Why is she never around when I need her?"

Marco looked up in surprise. "I didn't think anyone survived."

Cicero looked at him. "How quickly you forget, youngling. Remember what you saw at the end."

Marco shuddered, remembering the horrifying scene of the cats clinging to Akeel as he stepped into the icy water.

"Now you know the story of how cats became the Guardians of the Books."

Marco thought had he lived in that time, Cicero would have been a Guardian Cat, not just an ordinary library cat. Marco blinked once, then again, as the truth dawned on him. Cicero *was* a Guardian.

"That's what's in the box downstairs!" he shouted.

Cicero kept climbing.

"It's Akeel's book, isn't it?" Marco badgered him from behind.

No answer.

"Come on, Cicero. Take me back down there to see it."

"Patience, Marco. My bones are weary and I need to rest. I must warn you, however. This has to remain secret. You can't tell a soul."

"The book can't be in danger now. Not here."

Cicero stopped and turned again. "The Professor is one who will never give up his quest for power. Hope that he never finds his way here."

Professor? What Professor? It seemed like all of Cicero's explanations only raised more questions.

Alaniah fluttered around their heads. "Silly cats. I am never far away." She opened the portal and Marco breathed the welcoming smell of books as they stepped through the mirror into the library.

"I am going to go rest now, but I would like you to meet the others."

"Others?"

"I haven't told you about the other readers, have I?"

"Readers? You mean reader cats?"

"Midnight tomorrow, behind the Café Ole. Come to a meeting of the Dead Cats Society."

DUMPSTER CATS

I t was the dead of night in the parking lot behind the Café Ole. The lot was empty. So empty, that for a while Marco wondered if he had the wrong place or the wrong time, but gradually a few strays straggled in.

"You're not from around here, are you?" accused a wind-blown cat with bug eyes. Marco tried to hold his tongue.

"Speak up, stranger! Make yourself known," the hostile cat retorted.

"Easy there," said a sleek gray cat, just coming in.

"You causing trouble again, Skitzo?" asked a scraggly tom missing one eye.

"Everyone knows the rules. We have to be careful who we let in. And don't call me Skitzo. It's not my real name."

"What *is* your real name, Skitzo?" asked the biggest cat Marco had ever seen.

Skitzo mumbled something no one could understand.

The big cat, a Maine Coon, turned to Marco. "Skitzo tells us his owner inserted a chip in his head."

"Former owner, thank goodness. But it's true! They're using it to track me."

"Why would they want to track you, Skitzo? You're so mean."

The aristocratic gray introduced himself to Marco more formally. "Excuse our bad manners. My name is Bait. It's short for Baitengirth, but I rarely use my royal name."

Marco had never met royalty and liked his polished manner. Better than the others, he thought.

"You got something to hide?" asked Skitzo, not wanting to drop his challenge. "Out with it."

"Show some manners," said Bait. "We should treat our guests more graciously. Now, how about a civilized introduction. You are…?"

"I'm Marco."

"Marco," muttered Skitzo. "Wasn't he some kind of spy?"

"Boy, you should read more, Skitzo. Marco was a famous explorer, not a spy," said the scruffy tomcat.

"Well, Marco, you know who Skitzo is," continued Bait. "This is Tweezer, that's Pudge and over there is Gypsy with her kittens."

A long-haired white Persian sauntered in. "Anyone seen my book? I stashed it here last meeting. Now I can't find it anywhere."

"You mean that stupid fashion magazine, Caffeina?" asked Tweezer. "That's not a book!"

"Well, it's a lot better than your biker magazines." The white cat swished her tail in Tweezer's face and strolled off.

This is not what Marco expected. Was this some kind of joke Cicero was playing on him?

For all their grumbling, the arguments didn't get physical. They scattered out and a few of them disappeared into a large dumpster to search for food scraps from the restaurant.

Marco investigated the surroundings. Metal trashcans and empty food boxes lined the back of the brick restaurant. He sniffed lettuce, rotten bananas and dead potted plants. It seemed a waste of time, and he decided to leave.

"Seize the day!" cried a familiar voice.

Marco jumped, along with the others.

Cicero had arrived unnoticed and taken his place on the wooden crate he used as a podium.

"Greetings, fellow Readers," he announced, unable to hide the fact that he was enjoying the small bit of drama caused by his arrival.

But the drama was short-lived. Now they just seemed bored, licking French fry grease off their paws.

STAGE FRIGHT

Cicero sighed. He was well aware his passion for sharing Guardian stories was met with mixed enthusiasm. While they found the idea exciting and a few even dreamed of someday becoming a Guardian, none of these cats had what it took. Still, it was part of his duty to maintain the tradition of the Dead Cats Society as—what was that strange term? Social outreach?

Cicero gave the cats time to finish their grooming. All were homeless, although they didn't think of themselves as strays. They'd had humans somewhere in their past, for better or worse.

All were tough survivors, though. Tweezer was a drop-off at Mrs. Wilcox's Cat Rescue Mission, and Gypsy had strong barn cat lineage. He knew Skitzo stayed on the move, lurking behind markets and cafés, skittish of human contact, but Pudge was only too happy to have the café owner for a friend. Marco liked to sleep in tall trees or rooftops, when weather permitted.

Then there was Caffeina, of whom he felt some fatherly affection. She told the others she lived at the

Fairmont Hotel, and he never let on that it was a janitorial closet at the Sleep N'Go Motel.

He spotted Bait making small talk with Marco. He knew the most about him; a pedigreed Russian Blue, born at a breeding cattery and adopted by a woman who supplied him with pricy collars, toys and food.

Bait was proud of the awards he won at cat shows and how well he'd learned to read in the long hours he spent alone at home. He favored psychology journals. A strange choice, thought Cicero, but then Bait was a strange cat.

Bait told him he grew bored with the cat shows, and shortly after, a white Persian kitten appeared in his house. They despised each other from the start. When Bait drew blood on the kitten's face, the woman threw him outside, and that was that.

The important thing was that somewhere along the way, this little group had all acquired the ability to read. It was rapidly becoming a lost art, and so, even if they didn't read the best stuff, they came faithfully to meetings.

Gypsy kept him supplied with kittens to tutor, and they were his hope for the future. Reader cats were necessary to maintain the tradition of passing on the Guardian Cat stories.

It was the next Guardian Cat he was worried about. He must be sure this time.

"What's your story about tonight, Cicero?" asked Lily.

Lily and Sophie, two of Gypsies kittens, were always eager for his stories.

Tonight I will tell you the story of a Guardian Cat named Gadiel. He lived long ago in the frozen steppes of the Ural Mountains. That's in western Russia."

"Hey, Cicero," interrupted Skitzo. "What are you gonna do about this stray? I thought we had rules."

"Yeah, like you live by the rules, Skitzo," countered Caffeina.

"Yeah, like you're not a stray," said Tweezer, the tomcat.

Skitzo ignored them and pushed his point with Cicero. "The one who calls himself Marco. What happened to security around here? Shouldn't he at least swear by the Code?"

"We'll get around to that in good time," replied Cicero patiently.

"Like… ?" pushed Skitzo.

Cicero tolerated Skitzo's rudeness. He didn't expect much in the way of manners from the strays, but he did enjoy teasing them.

"Okay, Skitzo. Maybe you're right," he said.

Skitzo looked smugly at the others.

"In fact, now is the perfect time. Why don't you recite it for us?"

Skitzo looked like a deer caught in a car's headlights.

"Way to go, Skitzo! You stepped in that one," yelled Tweezer.

"I can recite it," offered Lily. "I've been memorizing it this week. Mum's teaching me."

"Okay, Lily. Let's hear it."

Skitzo, under his breath, mumbled, "Bootlicker."

"Psycho," Lily snapped back and scampered up to the front. In her small, confident voice, she began. "I will now recite the Code of the Dead Cats Society... a society created by our beloved Guardian Cats to help promote the cause of reading and other higher pursuits."

She took a deep breath. "I swear that I will put the welfare of others before my own..." She trailed off and looked to Cicero for help.

"Interests," he coached.

"Oh, yeah. I swear that I will endeavor to uphold honor in the face of cor-por-a-tions..."

"Corruption," corrected Cicero, smiling.

"Co-rup-shun. Okay. Uh, where was I? I will seek to be courageous in the face of danger. I will seek to live at peace with others, but never, uh..."

"Hesitate."

"Yes, never hesitate to defend the weak and helpless against the forces of evil and injustice." In her softest voice, she said, "I will aim to be gentle spoken and not boastful of my good deeds." Then she lifted her head and pushed out her chest, raising the pitch of her voice again. "And I will remain true to my word and loyal to the ideals and principles of the Dead Cats Society."

"Well done, Lily! Thank you," said Cicero. He turned to Marco. "Lily's mum can help you learn the Code. I'm sure you will have it memorized in no time. Now, we usually have a Reader share something before I begin my story. Skitzo keeps us posted on tabloid news. Pudge reads from Garfield comics and Caffeina keeps us well supplied with the latest gossip from *Cat Fashion*."

"Oh. Wow," said Marco, trying not to appear stunned.

"You are reading an adventure, right? Why don't you tell us about it."

"Oh… maybe next time."

"There's no time like the present," Cicero gently insisted.

Marco threaded his way through Gypsy's newest batch of kittens. She spoke encouragingly to him. "Don't worry. You'll do fine. The first time is the hardest."

All the cats were staring at him. Marco hung his head. He'd never had to give a book report before.

"A little stage fright? Don't worry, we've all been there," Cicero said. "How about starting with the name of the book?"

He didn't think this crowd would be much interested in his book, but he took a deep breath and plowed ahead. "*The Three Musketeers*," he said in a hoarse voice.

"Can't hear you," said Skitzo.

Marco looked at Cicero, who nodded to him. "*The Three Musketeers,*" Marco repeated in a stronger voice.

"The three what?" asked Caffeina.

"Musketeers. They're like soldiers."

"Okay, go on. Tell us what you like about the book," Cicero said.

"Well, I do like the hero in the story," Marco began uneasily, and then suddenly, the words came spilling out of him. "His name is d'Artagnan and he lived in the time of the French King, Louis the Thirteenth. He was rather a reckless and bold sort of fellow and managed to get himself into all sorts of predicaments." Marco smiled, remembering how much he loved the book. "As soon as he arrived in Paris, he was challenged to a duel by three musketeers, and then their duel is interrupted and all of them had to fight the Cardinal's guards, and..."

"Awesome!" Callema was gazing fondly at Marco. The others all had a glazed look in their eyes.

Marco washed his face, stalling for time, but he didn't have to worry about facing the rude alley cats any longer. Something much bigger had invaded.

BLACK MASKS AND ATTITUDE

They had black masks and attitude—raccoons, they must have been, although none of the cats had ever encountered a live one. There were only three, but their presence was intimidating and the cats had their hackles up.

"Did I say you could eat outta my dumpsta'?" said the biggest varmint, a disreputable looking raccoon with a deep scar on one ear.

The Dead Cats growled and hissed, but no one responded to the senseless question.

Except Tweezer. "Who do you think you are?"

"Oh, excu-use me. I didn't know we needed intra-ductions. This is my territory, so ya better get used to me, ya mangy felines. Name's Sting. Don't forget it!"

All three raccoons had banded eyes, but Sting's were particularly narrow and his wide mouth flaunted no-nonsense fangs.

Before Tweezer could reply, Lily piped up. "I don't think so! We eat here all the time, so it's our dumpster, mister, not yours. Besides, you're interrupting our meeting."

Sting was dumbfounded, probably for the first time in his life

"Yeah, pip-squeak? A meetin'? What kinda meetin' do a bunch 'a cats have?"

"We are the Dead Cats Society, I'll have you know," Lily blurted out.

Jaws dropped and the crowd fell silent.

"Dead cats?" Sting suddenly looked worried. "You's are dead?"

"No, but *you* might be if you don't scram!" yelled Tweezer.

"Right, I'm scared now. How 'bout you boys? You scared? Tank? Crimmany?" Sting asked his two cohorts.

"We're shaking in our boots, boss."

"Sooo's what do a bunch 'a dead cats do? Tell ghost stories?" laughed Sting.

"That's a good one, boss!" said Tank.

Lily explained, "We read."

"Huh?"

"Read. You know, books."

"You read *what?*"

"You don't know what a book is, mister?"

"I know what a book is!" said Crimmany, obviously the runt of the gang.

"Shut up! Course I know what a book is. You think I'm stupid or somethin'?"

"I think you're brain dead, that's what I think!" Caffeina chimed in.

Not wanting to be left out of the argument, Skitzo pushed forward through the cats and declared, "This is a top secret meeting. If you don't leave now, I'm callin' the cops."

"A secret meetin'?" asked Sting. "Ri-ight. You must be undercover cats and this is your secret hiding place... by the trash cans. I'm so impressed."

"You have no idea who we are," said Cicero. "So take your buddies and go find another dumpster."

"And who might you be, ol' man?" Sting asked. "You somebody I should be takin' orders from?"

"You leave him alone!" said Pudge.

Bait tried a diplomatic approach. "I'm sure you don't want a fight. Please let us continue with our meeting. There are other trash bins down the road."

Sting, undoubtedly the lead gangster raccoon, was never diplomatic. "Boys," he said, without looking at his co-conspirators. "We gots ourselves a sit-u-a-shun."

With more grace than one would expect, the jumbo-sized raccoon swooped up Lily, the petite kitten who had so boldly challenged him. He held her out at arm's length, as if she were a smelly sock. "Hey, kitty. How 'bout readin' to Uncle Sting?"

Lily hung limply in his grasp.

"Not talkin', huh?" Sting yelled, shaking her like a rag doll. "Then I'll take you home with me. You can read to me there. Come on, Tank, Crimmany. Let's go."

The Dead Cats had not been idle—they had positioned themselves for an attack. Four of them leaped directly at Sting. Gypsy, Lily's mother, bit him on the leg, and Bait tried to block him. Pudge, the only one who came close in size to Sting, succeeded in knocking him briefly on his back.

Marco had climbed up the dumpster to gain some height and used the vantage point to take a nosedive, striking Sting directly in his midsection. It would have been an effective move, if Marco had been bigger. As it was, he simply bounced off the fat-bellied raccoon and landed on the pavement. Marco, who'd never said anything mean, couldn't help but mutter 'Fatso' under his breath. Sting took a swipe at him but missed.

"You morons. You think you can take me on?" growled Sting, still clutching Lily. "You're nuthin' more than pets. You should all be curled up on somebody's lap." He called out to his crew, "Boys, get a move on!"

"Whatcha gonna do with the kitten, Boss?"

"I'm takin' it with me. Maybe it's time ol' Sting had his own pet," said Sting.

The raccoons scurried off towards the alley, and in a bold move, Tweezer plunged down from the back of a parked truck and sunk his teeth into Sting's arm before he could get away.

Lily dropped, coming to consciousness, and landed on her feet. Before Sting could make a countermove, Marco grabbed Lily by the scruff of her neck—not a move that comes natural to a male cat—and awkwardly dashed off, putting enough distance between her and her kidnappers to keep her safe.

Sting left in a huff, hurling a warning. "You'll be sorry, you scabby cats. Don't think you've seen the last of me!"

"WE ARE SUCH STUFF AS DREAMS ARE MADE ON..."

Marco's head hurt from thinking. Mostly he was thinking about the mystery that was Cicero. How could he imagine that time traveling was just 'a little trip'? Why did he waste his time teaching illiterate strays? Who *was* he? Sometimes he seemed so old, lost in research that had no real-world implications. Then other times, Marco felt like Cicero was leading him down a dangerous path—one that was very real.

Then there was the annoying side of the old library cat. Cicero insisted he attend the Dead Cats meetings. What a joke. Those cats were more interested in eating and fighting than reading. He could not imagine them spending any time in a library and didn't see how they could be guardians of anything. Well, maybe Bait. Bait was different from the others.

But then, ever since returning from Alexandria, nothing seemed the same and after his disastrous first meeting, all he wanted was a good book in a quiet corner of the library.

But that was the problem. Here he was in his favorite place, and even though it sounded quiet, it didn't feel quiet. He blamed Cicero.

Marco quit trying to read and went upstairs. The old cat was busy pouring through the stack of books in his chambers and Alaniah was playing around, doing swoops and dives and generally amusing herself. Marco went in, hoping to get an answer to his biggest 'why' question, but Cicero kept on reading.

Marco tried to be patient, but the more Cicero ignored him, the more important the question became.

Alaniah swooped and hovered in a holding pattern above Marco. "You ask good questions, fledgling-ing," she said.

"How do you know my question?"

"I can hear the thoughts of creatures... when I choose. Mostly they are not so interesting as yours." She looked towards Cicero. "Impossible to get his attention when he's researching, isn't it?" She waved several of her wings in dismissal. "You want to know why he didn't warn them, don't you?"

"He could have saved so many lives! He could have saved the library," Marco protested. "Instead, he just let it happen!"

"This is difficult for you, and it is hard for me to see time from your perspective. Worldly creatures, such as you-ou," she said, her voice rising with a touch of superiority, "observe time as past, present and future. But it is not so simple. Time is such a limiting dimension-ion... but unfortunately you earth creatures are stuck with it."

Alaniah twirled her ethereal sparkliness upwards and sailed around the room as though even the thought of being tethered by three dimensions was something to be avoided at all costs.

Cicero finally looked up from his books.

"Ah, there he is," she said. "Now you may explain. I cannot even fathom what it must be like for you, imprisoned in heavy corporeal bodies, plodding along in a time continuum-um."

"Oh Alaniah, we are who we are," said Cicero. "To quote a great man, 'We are such stuff as dreams are made on.'" But at least we cats do not face the same limitations as humans. We are able to time travel and see into other dimensions much easier. Well, I have to qualify that. Cats *used* to have this ability, but even they are losing it, just as they are losing the ability to read."

He looked at Marco directly. "But to your question, Marco… about why I didn't save the library or warn Akeel."

Cicero *had* been listening after all.

"All I can tell you is when we travel back in time, we are only observers. We cannot affect what has happened in the past. We cannot even be seen by most of the inhabitants."

"What about Akeel? He saw us."

"Akeel and Chuluum were different. They were given the gift to see what others could not."

"But why couldn't you give him some small hint? What's the point of going back if you can't change anything?"

"There is much speculation about time traveling. Humans are fascinated with this subject as well, thinking that they can change something that has already happened in the past to make life better in the present. However, as appealing as the idea is, it is not only not possible, it would be terribly dangerous."

"Dangerous. Don't you think the fire was dangerous?"

"As tragic as it was, changing things wouldn't necessarily make it better."

Marco did not see how things could have been worse.

"Careless use of time travel leads to rifts, a tear in the fabric of events. Even the slightest alteration would create an enormous wave that would sweep out over every event, before and after. When a pebble is tossed into a pond, ripples spread out into ever-widening circles. If a boulder were thrown in, a tidal wave of events would change everything around it, not just one small thing.

"No, it has not been granted to us mere mortals to have this kind of an effect on things that have already happened."

Marco was not sure that Cicero had answered his question. For that matter, he couldn't even remember the question. He had gotten lost at 'a tear in the fabric' and 'tossing of pebbles into a pond.'

He sighed, thinking he would never understand the kinds of things Cicero talked about, but he couldn't help asking questions. "Cicero, why are they called the 'dead cats'?"

FIRST LESSONS

Marco's question made Cicero feel as if he had awoken from a dream. He left his theories and complicated matters and went over to sit beside the young cat.

Marco showed promise as a future Guardian, but it was still too soon to be sure. He was young, naïve, impulsive and daring. Those qualities, in time, could develop into bravery and courage. He'd need that. But he'd seen how the same traits could be turned into reckless and untamed ambition.

"I've been negligent in instructing you—putting the cart before the horse, I believe is the saying. It's time you learned something about the Guardian Cats."

They both settled into sunny spots on the window sill.

"I will start with the Guardian called Adelphos. One of the places Akeel found was a deserted farmhouse on the outskirts of a small Greek fishing village. Adelphos was one of the many Guardian Cats there.

"During the day, he wandered through flower and fish markets, keeping their stalls free of mice. The fish vendors and food merchants all saved him special treats, each one thinking that Adelphos loved him best.

Cicero saw Marco was drowsy from the warm sun, but as usual, Marco's tummy growled whenever food was mentioned, and Cicero was glad to have his full attention.

"Adelphos began tutoring kittens who gathered every day at the markets, telling them stories of past Guardian Cats and teaching them how to read. It had been Akeel's inspiration to have the Guardian Cats pass on the stories. The tutoring part was added to teach humility to our prideful natures and Adelphos was the first cat who took up the challenge.

"A cat's only shortcoming," said Cicero, "is the one of being too proud." He chuckled at the irony of his own statement. "Community service to the less fortunate was Akeel's idea as a remedy for curing this weakness of ours. The name 'dead cats' was coined by Gaspar, one of Adelphos' students. If the discussions were getting too serious and he was in the mood for an old Guardian story, he would shout out, 'Let's hear a tale about one of those dead cats!'"

Marco's eyes lit up with delight.

"Some of the others still don't get the joke," said Cicero, pleased with his student's ability to grasp subtle humor.

"But we have more pressing concerns. The raccoons. What will we do about them? I don't think they will go away peacefully. What do you think Marco?" asked Cicero.

"I don't think they'll go away either. In fact, if we don't take care of them soon, we might become 'dead cats'.

Cicero couldn't hide his smile.

STING'S HEADQUARTERS

From a distance the pickup looked abandoned, but inside were signs of life. The raccoons had taken up residence in the '52 Dodge. The faded orange truck with an additional camper shell more than suited their needs.

Inside, Sting was fuming mad. "Those dirty, rotten fleabag cats! Thinkin' they can raid our territory and call us intruders?" He paced back and forth in the covered truck bed.

"How is it that a bunch of scrawny alley cats managed to thrash you, Sting? You're not losing your touch, are you?" Tank asked.

Sting drew his large paw back and sent Tank flying. "Does it *feel* like I'm losin' my touch?"

"Sorry, boss. My mistake."

Sting sneered. Tank looked tough, but he was spineless. A chuckle coming from the outside interrupted them. Sting swung around. A small raccoon poked his head into the doorway.

"What's so funny?" Sting demanded.

"I was wondering how a mangy tomcat beat up a tough guy like you. And he's only half your size," replied the stranger.

"We was wondering about that, too," said Crimmany, boldly first, before he cringed.

Sting ignored him and glared at the intruder. "You callin' me fat?"

"Absolutely not. In fact, I envy your fine stature. Allow me to introduce myself. They call me Lazer," he said. "I've been spying on the cats for some time now." He chuckled. "It's sort of a hobby of mine."

"Oh yeah?" Sting started to warm up a little. He hadn't always hated felines, but the 'dead cats' made his skin crawl. Up until now he rarely gave cats a second thought. They always scattered when he took over their territory and never caused him any further trouble. Until now.

"The leader, Cicero, he's got some special kind of power. The others, they're just plain mean and ornery. But they're 'reader cats'," said Lazer, scrunching his nose, indicating the cats might have some contagious disease. "It makes them peculiar."

"I noticed that."

"Perhaps you'd be interested in where they get their power?" Lazer asked.

Sting smiled. Now here was a brother raccoon that actually might be useful to him.

No Mercy

On his way to the Lost and Embedded Manuscripts conference at the Library of Alexandria, Professor Chin took his planned layover in Greece. He was not there for sightseeing. A silent man nodded to him at the Athens airport and whisked him off to a smaller airport, where they boarded a private plane to the island of Rhodes. From Rhodes, a powerful skiff jetted them to a small remote island. In hardly any more time than it usually took to retrieve his luggage at Heathrow, he was sitting in the living room of Dr. Warner. He declined the offer of a drink.

He knew everyone here. They'd been meeting for five years and they were the closest to a family he would ever have. But by the end of the meeting, Professor Chin knew he wouldn't be coming back. He wasn't looking for a family. These men talked too much; they were too soft. And he was looking to do more than world building; their ideas would never be more than a fantasy. His, he knew, could be real. And people would pay the ultimate price for his world.

He needed men attuned to great leaders, like Hitler. Like Himmler. He would be the Grandmaster. Under his breath, he whispered Himmler's favorite word, 'gnadelos', no mercy.

THE LIBRARY OF ALEXANDRIA

The first thing that surprised Professor Chin about Alexandria was how modern it was. It was a bit disconcerting to be surrounded by foreigners—but what did he expect? He was pleased that everyone knew English, surprisingly well.

The second thing he learned was that, in this Mediterranean coastal city, he was overdressed in his tweed coat. He never went anywhere without his coat and umbrella. Reluctantly, he left both in his hotel room and joined the tour group, feeling slightly underdressed.

The third thing he discovered was that the new Library of Alexandria was jarring to his senses. He didn't bother to browse the stacks. His love for books wasn't like the love of a bibliophile. That was something he always had to be careful of at work, not letting on that books were only a means to an end.

The architectural lines of the ultramodern library were at odd angles, which threw him off balance. It's open, soaring lines made him small and insignificant. In London, he was always surrounded by a sense of the solidness of it. Here, he was out of his element, out of control.

He rubbed one hand over the other, massaging his fingers and wrist, something he'd done to relieve anxiety since he was a boy.

He was so distracted that he almost missed the next exhibit. The tour guide was talking about the historic burning of the original library. They were standing in front of a bronze statue of a young man in a tunic. There were bronze cats climbing all over him. "Nothing remains of the ancient library," the girl said, "but legends. This is Akeel, the Guardian librarian who, it is said, saved seven powerful mystical books, which were sheltered in secret chambers under the main buildings. He escaped the fire with a handful of books and an armful of library cats. When he found new hiding places for the books, he put the cats in charge of guarding them. As Egyptians, who revere cats, this story holds special charm for us." She smiled at the group and there were murmurs of appreciation. "The books are shrouded in mystery, but the legend says that whoever finds them and unlocks their secrets will be able to rule the world."

Professor Chin thought he was going to be sick. He struggled to hear more of what she said about the books, but he was feeling faint.

The thought of having cats crawling over him like the man in the statue made him nauseous. Gypsies believed cats were filthy creatures, if not downright evil. But when he was too small to know better, he had befriended one and always saved scraps of food from his evening meal.

When his stepfather caught him feeding the kitten, he beat him, then forced his mother to drown the cat, making him watch. He still remembered him yelling '*dinili!*', stupid, and how the cat scratched his mother's arms and face as she struggled to force the kitten's head into a bucket of water. "You think we have enough to feed a filthy cat when we can barely feed ourselves?" his stepfather had shouted.

He started trembling. He'd had nightmares about his cat coming back to life to punish him. In one dream, there were a dozen cats climbing all over him and he woke up screaming as one tried to suck the breath out of him.

Now he was looking at this statue of his nightmare while the people around him were obviously enjoying it.

He desperately wanted to avoid a panic attack but it was too late. The tour guide, an attractive young Arab girl, asked him if he was ok as the room started to spin and he reached out for something to hold onto.

The last thing he heard was the snickers of school children. When he woke up, he was lying on the floor and a paramedic was taking his blood pressure, a crowd standing over him. He passed out again.

Later, when he woke up the second time, he was in his hotel room, thankful to be away from people. But he wasn't alone.

"What was that all about?" demanded the Whisperer.

"Nevermind."

"Nevermind! What is the matter with you?" demanded the Whisperer. "You'll never get anywhere falling apart like that!"

"Have a little sympathy," said Professor Chin. "Maybe it was something I ate."

"Sympathy! You're one to ask for sympathy. Am I wasting my time with you?"

"No. I'll be fine. You heard what she said, didn't you? You were there?"

"You mean about the books?"

"Of course, I mean about the books."

"What about them? It's just a story."

"You don't believe that any more than I do. These kinds of things exist. You know about the Spear of Destiny, don't you? It was the tool for Hitler's power. These books will be my Spear."

"How badly do you want them?"

"With all my soul."

"I have my resources," said the Whisperer, after some considering. "I could have them look for the books. But I must warn you. They expect a steep price for their services."

"Any price is worth increasing my powers."

"You would give your soul for a magical book?"

"What need have I of my soul? It causes me only pain. Take what's left of it. What I need, my soul won't give me. What I need is power."

POLO'S DANGEROUS DISCOVERY

"**M**arco, where have you been?" demanded Polo. Marco was climbing down the wide trunk of the tree next to the ferrets' home, his usual spot, except for nights when he fell asleep at the library. Cicero had implied that the staff might not want a second library cat, so he always had to scurry out the window when the librarians opened up in the morning.

To be sure, he hadn't been around much lately, as he was spending more and more time at the library. He hadn't told Polo about his other life, because... he wasn't sure why. It was just a feeling, but he figured Polo would want to tag along with him and he didn't think the library was ready for the likes of a silly ferret.

Still, Marco felt a little guilty about keeping secrets from his new friend. Polo bounced and leaped and ran circles around Marco. "I've been looking all over for you!

"What's the matter? What's going on?"

"Nothing. I missed you."

"Oh, Polo! I'm sorry." Marco felt badly about ignoring him. "I'm not trying to avoid you or anything. It's just that I have things I need to do."

This statement from his cat friend stopped the little ferret for a moment. "Oh well," said Polo, shrugging it off. "You're here now! I can show you my new treasure!" he cried out. "It's my most beautiful possession!"

He ran under the house and reappeared with a silver keychain attached to a tube of liquid. "Look! It's got water inside."

Marco leaned in closer to the tube. "It doesn't smell like water, Polo. It's awful." Marco jerked his head back and crinkled his nose at the biting odor. The red tube was about half-full of liquid.

"That's disgusting. What do you want it for?"

"It goes with my red jewelry collection. Look here! See the little wheel?"

Marco did not like Polo's latest stolen good. Lucy's father had one almost like it. He recognized it by the smell. It was a flame shooter.

FINDERS KEEPERS

Marco escaped back to the tree while Polo loped across the weedy backyard, the cigarette lighter dangling from his mouth, and crawled through a fence hole into the neighbor's yard.

A tire swing swayed gently in the evening breeze, and the promise of hidden spaces lured the ferret. He dropped the lighter and pulled himself up into the rubbery den, exploring pretty much everything there was to see inside a tire. When he heard voices, he stood straight up and looked out through the wide hole. There were three large animals with black masks sniffing their way around a bunch of kid's plastic toys. He recognized their bandit faces. Raccoons.

"We're being watched," said one of them, suddenly noticing Polo. "Look'it that varmint in the hangin' tire. What is it?"

"Looks like a deformed rat, don't you think?" said another.

"Who, or should I say, what are you?" asked the biggest one.

Polo felt no obligation to explain himself and ignored their comparing him to a rat. It happened all the time.

"In case you haven't heard, we own this part of town now. My name's Sting and these are my two fine young companions."

Even though a vagabond and a thief, Polo was completely devoid of cruel intentions, and he did not recognize a bully for what he was.

"You deaf or something?" asked Sting. "You gotta be, with those puny ears."

"Yeah, deaf and dumb," said Tank.

Polo had had enough. He drew in a breath. "Hey, bugle ears!" he yelled. "You're hurtin' my eyes. How come you're so fat?"

"No one talks to me like that!" Sting said, and before Polo could blink, he was yanked out of the tire by his neck and tossed to the ground.

Polo was undeterred. He raised himself to his fullest height, bared his teeth and challenged Sting with his fiercest look.

Just as Sting was about to take another swipe at him, the smallest raccoon ran up.

"Hey, Sting! Take a look at this!" He handed him the cigarette lighter.

"My, my," said Sting. "This *is* interesting."

"Hey, that's mine!" Polo yelled.

"Shut up," said Sting. "This here trinket might save your life if you was smart enough to keep your trap shut."

Polo had no intention of letting it go. He tried grabbing the lighter, but Sting seized him by the throat until his eyes bulged and the lighter fell out of his hand gone limp.

DAVID AND GOLIATH

Scuffling noises from the ground woke Marco from his nap. Through the tree branches he saw three large animals scavenging plastic kid's toys in the yard next door.

"Nothing here worth eatin', boss," said one.

He recognized them immediately, but he was in no mood for another fight with raccoons. Besides, they weren't hurting anything and they'd never notice him. He curled up to resume his nap, when all of the sudden, there was Polo in the middle of the raccoons—nabbed right out of a tire swing and thrown to the ground.

He saw Polo rise from the dust and face his assailant, like David defying Goliath.

But Marco knew Polo wouldn't stand a chance in a battle with these thugs and skittered rapidly down the tree and through the fence hole.

"What the….?" Sting said, shocked.

Marco was quickly flanked by Sting's two cohorts. They peered at him through their black masks.

"Hey, isn't he one of those dead cats, Sting?"

"You're about to be a dead raccoon," countered Marco. "Let him go!"

Polo was squirming in Sting's grip.

"Sure thing, buddy. Tank. Crimmany. You know what to do." Sting tossed Polo aside.

All three raccoons launched themselves at Marco. One bit his tail and Marco whirled around, smacking him with claws extended. Next thing he knew though, he was at the bottom of the heap. He clawed furiously, tasting dirt and blood. Then... pain pierced his body, first his ear, then his nose. He could barely breathe.

His saving grace came from pure instinct, a cat trick he didn't know he had until he needed it. He jerked his body like a corkscrew, twisting his bones inside his loose skin. Free from the vicious bullies, he darted up the tree and watched the raccoons claw at each other until they discovered he had disappeared.

The raccoons, dazed and confused, rummaged around for a minute.

"I hate cats," said Sting. "They're freakin' me out. Let's scram."

"Hey Sting, you still want this?" asked Crimmany, holding up Polo's lighter.

"Sure, you never know. It might come in handy."

WILD DISREGARD FOR ORDER

For security reasons, Cicero moved the Dead Cats meetings from the Café parking lot to a room inside the library—a storage area where the window was permanently stuck open. Not that any librarian could even see the window, let alone get to it.

The room was crammed so full there was no pathway left for people. Wooden card catalogs took up half the space. A large bust of Mark Twain kept company with an ancient manual typewriter on an overstuffed chair. Piles of cardboard boxes, books and magazines looked as though they'd given up their struggle for organization and succumbed to the gravity of neglect.

Cicero thought it was perfect. The room had the right balance of coziness and wild disregard for order.

Already most of the cats had found something of interest. Gypsy browsed through *Mothering Magazine* while her kittens pounced over her. Skitzo was reading an article in the *Daily Observer* titled "Missing Baby Found Inside Watermelon!" Caffeina looked bored as she flipped the pages of *Cat Diva*.

Heads raised as Marco climbed into the room through the narrow window opening, his ear and nose torn, dried blood on his tail.

Caffeina was the first to jump up. "Mee-oow! Marco, what happened to you?"

Tweezer asked, "Who won?"

Marco held his head and tail high, battle scars and all. "I did pretty well, considering," he said proudly.

"Considering....?"

"Considering the face-off Polo and I had with the raccoons."

"Raccoons!"

"Who did you say you were with?" asked Skitzo.

"My friend, Polo."

Tweezer came closer and examined Marco's injuries. "Did you leave your mark on them?" he asked.

"They won't soon forget me," said Marco.

"Who's Polo?" Skitzo insisted, peering suspiciously at Marco.

"He's a friend."

"Do we know him?"

"Not exactly," answered Marco.

Skitzo circle Marco, inspecting him like an interrogator. "Why doesn't he come to meetings?"

"I thought it was just for cats."

"What? He's not a cat?" asked Skitzo, appalled.

"Well... no," Marco said. "Polo's a... well, he's a ferret."

Dead silence.

"A what?" asked Sophie, who was never afraid to admit when she didn't know something.

"A ferret."

"You have a friend who's not a cat?" challenged Skitzo.

"You're repeating yourself Skitzo. A sure sign of psycho-ness. Anyway, so what?" said Caffeina. "No law says we can't be friends with other species. I have a good friend who's a dog."

"You should be careful who you're friends with, Caffeina."

"That's funny, coming from you Skitzo. Since you don't have *any* friends," retorted the cheeky feline.

"Here. Here," interjected Cicero. "Marco, inform the others about ferrets."

Marco wasn't sure how to describe a ferret to a cat. "He has fur, but he doesn't look much like us. He's long, hardly any ears, and…" What could he tell them?

The cats were waiting.

Then he remembered what he liked most about his friend. "Ferrets are funny. At least Polo's funny," he blurted out.

"Oh!"

It was the perfect answer for the cats and broke the tension. For most of them, anyway.

"Funny is overrated," said Skitzo. "I can't remember the last time I was funny."

"That's because you've never been funny," countered Caffeina.

"You risked your life for a ferret?" asked Bait.

"Well, yeah. I mean, I didn't stop to think about it," said Marco. "Polo's my friend. I had to defend him."

"Very noble of you," replied Bait.

"How many did you say there were?" asked Cicero.

"Three. The same thugs who broke into our meeting."

"You fought all three by yourself and lived to tell about it?" asked Pudge.

There was an admiring squeal from Caffeina. "Three raccoons on your own! You're a hero!"

Had Marco been human, he would have been blushing.

"I think we should meet this friend of yours," Bait said. "This one who inspires so much loyalty."

"Yes! You should bring him to a meeting," agreed Pudge.

Marco was relieved they were willing to meet Polo, especially since he was waiting outside.

Polo's head shot up in the window. "Can I come in now? It's boring out here." Without waiting for an answer, he leaped through and fell on the floor. He picked himself up and looked around. It didn't take long for him to decide who was having the most fun, and he immediately joined in with the kittens.

The older cats stared in group silence at the odd creature frolicking with the little ones. Gypsy broke the silence. "Guys. Focus. The raccoons. We can't keep ignoring this problem by hiding."

"The raccoons are cramping *my* lifestyle, that's for sure," said Pudge. "They come over every night and raid the dumpster. And would you believe? The human who used to feed me... she thinks the raccoons are cute! Now they get all the scraps. They're such pigs!"

Cicero tried to calm them down. "Raccoons don't stay in one place long. They're drifters, so I believe they'll move on soon. For now, we need to lie low."

"Great! We have to skulk around while they terrorize the neighborhood?" Skitzo asked, his voice rising.

"We could turn them in to Animal Control," suggested Caffeina. "Those guys are always picking up stray dogs in my neighborhood."

"Oh, you're so brilliant, Caffeina," Tweezer said, rolling his eyes. "How are we going to do *that*? You know some human who understands 'cat'? "

THE LONDON BOOKSHOP

The dull ache in his hind leg woke Cicero and the bittersweet memories came flooding back.

He missed Amelia. He missed the labyrinthine maze of books and magazines in her bookshop, the cafés on London's narrow cobblestone street behind the store, the treats he always found waiting for him.

He even missed dodging the shoes one merchant threw at him and the excitement of never knowing when a motor scooter would come charging down the alley like some avenging angel.

When he greeted Amelia's customers, they'd exclaim, "Oh, you're the cat on the mews!" and laugh hysterically. He never understood what was so funny.

His last day at the bookstore, he had been lying in a sunny patch by the front window. Something in the air changed the moment the man stepped into the shop.

A gray fedora shadowed his face. He wore a tweed coat and carried a satchel which weighed down one shoulder.

"Do you carry rare books?" he had asked Amelia, rubbing his hands together as if they were cold, even though the day was warm. Cicero remembered how his moustache bobbed as he spoke.

Before Amelia could answer, the man was talking again. "Ah, um, I should introduce myself. Where are my manners?" he said, fumbling in his pocket. He handed Amelia his card. "I'm Doctor Chin. But most people call me 'Professor'."

Amelia had seemed delighted with his presence, but she was like that with everyone. Cicero followed them as she guided the man on a tour of the small crowded bookstore. There should not be a shadow inside, he knew, but sure enough, one was following this man.

"Lovely shop, yes," the man said. "And I will browse through that art collection in the back, but I wonder if... I feel a little foolish asking." He laughed tightly. "Are there any hidden rooms?"

"You mean, like in the movies?" Amelia asked, her laugh generous and natural.

"Well, yes. Exactly. You know, a sliding door or revolving bookcase..."

"Oh, I don't think so, Professor. This is an ordinary bookshop."

Cicero moved protectively to Amelia's side.

"Nothing mysterious here. Right, Cicero?" She picked him up and cradled him in her arms.

The man jolted slightly.

"Oh! I hope you're not allergic to cats," said Amelia.

"Oh no, that's not it. I mean... he just surprised me, that's all."

The man's breathing quickened, but he insisted he wasn't allergic. They had stopped walking and were standing in front of a collection of children's picture books. Cicero could feel the man's loathing for him even as he said to Amelia, "Lovely cat. You had him long?"

"Cicero's been here since... well, since before I bought the place. Oh my, that's been over fifteen years."

Cicero glared at the man.

"Fifteen years! He doesn't appear that old," said the man. He had been backing slowly away from Amelia as he tried to keep up the conversation.

"Well, Cicero is an amazing cat. He's quite a fixture here. Everyone loves him."

"Hmmm, yes."

Cicero had never encountered a human who had taken an immediate dislike to him in such a strong way.

"He's an unusual looking cat. More spotted than striped, like an Egyptian Mau."

"Oh... I don't know what kind of cat he is. He's just my adorable Cicero."

"Do you know about the legendary cats of Iskandriyah?" The man was nervous, but Amelia didn't seem to notice.

"What?"

"Iskandriyah. Surely you've heard of the Library of Iskandriyah? Of course, you may only know it as Alexandria."

"Of course." The sudden stiffening of Amelia's arms wasn't the main reason Cicero jumped down. The strange shadow moved apart from the man. It seemed to have a life of its own.

"I think I've struck a nerve," said the man.

"Oh now, Professor. That's silly. He's just a cat."

"Such a nice cat."

Cicero glowered at him.

The bell over the door jingled, and Amelia seemed relieved. "Feel free to look around while I tend to my other customers."

Cicero tracked the Professor, who alternated between looking at books and making furtive taps on the walls.

"You look like a cat with something to hide," he said. "I thought the Guardian Cats were just a myth. Filthy creatures like you are good for nothing more than being a witch's familiar."

Cicero felt the man's struggle between desire and loathing for him. It would have made sense to turn and run, but his guardian instincts had kicked in.

"Is this the right place, this sorry excuse for a bookstore? How ironic that it's supposed to be in London, so close to home." The man seemed to be in conversation with someone else. "And why did you lead me here and not show me exactly where it is?" Who was he talking to?

"I paid dearly for this!" the man continued, his voice low and strained. "Don't even think of short changing me on our deal." The Professor seemed to be in conversation with the shadow.

Cicero kept his distance and breathed a sigh of relief when closing time finally came.

After Amelia locked up, he scooted through his cat door out into the alley to breathe the night air, but he was greeted with the tantalizing smell of fish.

How could he have known it was a trap? The instant he stepped over the wire, it snapped shut. Cicero went wild, throwing himself against the sides of the cage.

When he realized that an escape was impossible, he hunkered down, ignoring the fish. Out of the shadows the Professor spoke. "I knew you were more than just a sleepy shop cat."

Cicero hissed. How could this have happened? The Professor took him, cage and all, and put him in the trunk of his car. They drove a short while, the car stopped and the man carried him into a small room, where he was placed on a table.

"Don't worry. I don't want to become friends." He opened a suitcase and picked things out, setting them on the other end of the table.

"This should prove interesting. I've never tried this with a cat, but my mother's magic might have been good for something." He turned out the lights and lit a candle. Cicero stared at the man, who stared at the candle. First silently, then chanting, sometimes whispery, other times loudly, again talking to creatures even Cicero couldn't see.

Not at first.

Then one after another, dark shadows appeared on the walls, peeled off and entered the room, finding their places. One came and slithered into the cage, but Cicero hissed and spat so violently it backed off, emitting a snickering kind of laugh.

The Professor did not waver in his incantations. The candle flickered and sputtered, and more shadow creatures peeled off the walls. Then on the Professor's command, they merged and circled around his cage, absorbing the light.

They closed in on him and he struggled to breathe.

"Now let him go!" commanded Professor Chin, throwing his hands wide. The shadow creatures obeyed and slunk back into their corners. Cicero tried to stop shaking.

"I know who you are. Believe me, your days as Guardian are over. It's time to let someone have the book who can do it justice." He moved in close and Cicero took a swipe at him.

"Rethink your position, dear Cicero," pronouncing his name with disdain. "You can retire with all of your limbs intact. You will be able to sleep with both eyes shut. Your only other choice is to die a martyr's useless death."

Cicero resisted with all his might.

"Don't fight me!" commanded the Professor. "Tell me where the book is and I will let you go!"

For a fraction of a second, and against his will, Cicero's mind saw where it was hidden in the bookshop. He groaned. How could he have been so weak? He still cringed when he thought of that fateful moment.

"Yes!" the Professor exclaimed.

Cicero had not been able to prevent the Professor from penetrating his mind; it had been as captive as his body in the cage.

"Now show me the entryway."

Cicero felt his power weakening. Unable to resist the Professor's black magic, the tapestry covering the door under the stairs appeared as clear as anything in his mind. That was all the Professor needed.

"It's all coming back to me now. Mother always told me I had the gift. But I will go far beyond this weak gypsy magic. Tarot and tea leaves will not suffice. No one will ever have power over me now."

The Professor rubbed his hands together. Blocking the candle light, his shadow was thrown on the wall, looming larger than life.

As he talked, he began to unlatch the cage. "What a disgusting notion—cats guarding such a priceless treasure. This is not a book that should be hoarded in some forgotten bookstore by a filthy cat.

"Should I set you free? A gesture of good will, perhaps? I suppose there are men who might do such a thing, but I know the right way to treat a cat."

Cicero did not waste a moment. The instant the cage door was unlatched he became a wild animal and pushed through, leaping at the Professor and latching onto his neck.

The next thing he knew, he'd been hurled to the floor. All he could remember now from that moment was the numbness in his legs and disgrace in his soul.

After the Professor sped away in his car, a light appeared outside the doorway. Alaniah had arrived.

"Where have you been!" he scolded.

"I couldn't find you-ou. There was so much interference, my navigation system was thrown off.

However did you get to… what is this place? The Tar and Feathers Inn?"

"Never mind. There's no time to explain. I can't move, and I fear I've lost the book."

"Poor, dear Cicero. I'm so sorry. Lie still." Then Alaniah hovered above and showered him with something like warm snowflakes. Soon the feeling began to return to his leg.

"Make me a portal, Alaniah," he asked, and the Losring transported Cicero back to the bookshop. But it was too late. The tiny room had been ransacked. He went out the back and saw the man disappearing down the dark alleyway.

There was only one thing left for him to do. The power of the book was his to use in extreme circumstances. He hobbled down the alleyway, running as best he could on his three good legs, trying to imagine what in the world he would need to become in order to rescue the book.

As soon as the answer appeared, a wave of power surged through his body. Then his feet disappeared and outstretched wings emerged from his sides, lifting him off the cobblestone street and into the air.

The alley became his runway and he flew over the Professor's head, trying out his hawk wings. He soared in a wide circle, with the night sky and wind holding him above while he looked down at the earth from this new height.

The Professor left the alley for the street, dark and deserted except for one car and a few scattered pole lamps. Cicero's hawk eyes picked the target site and locked onto it, as though he'd done this a million times before.

The air whooshed under him as he picked up speed and made his silent, deadly descent. The Professor's hand was on the car door handle when he attacked, one jab with his beak in the darkest circle of the man's eye.

The Professor didn't make a sound right away. He fell to the ground, hugging his head, then let out one of the worst screams Cicero had ever heard coming out of a human. In one smooth motion, Cicero snatched the book with his talons and flew back up into the silent night sky.

DECISIONS

Cicero had never quite recovered from that experience. Alaniah had not wanted to take any chances going back to the bookstore and assured him she would find a safe place for them.

Not that he had any complaints about the sleepy Angel Springs library. The librarians let him have his own room where he read to his heart's content, but there were times when he still missed Amelia and the bookshop. Such are the hardships of a Guardian's life.

Today, especially, he was feeling his age. Few cats ever lived so long. Only those touched by a Losring like Alaniah. It was good to be blessed by such a creature, but for Guardian Cats it often meant they had not found their successor and needed more time. His pondering was interrupted by voices outside his chambers.

"I'll be good, I promise."

Cicero sighed. Why did he find the ferret creature so annoying?

Marco walked into the room and Polo came bursting in behind. He sat on his haunches, trying to imitate Marco.

"Greetings, Cicero," said Marco. "I brought Polo. I hope you don't min…"

"Well…" Cicero cut him off before he could finish.

"I want to learn how to read. Just like Marco!" Polo blurted out.

Cicero paused. *This* he was not expecting. "Hmm."

"I'm a fast learner."

Cicero did not feel like being diplomatic, but he held his tongue.

Polo did not hold his. "How about a story then? Marco says you tell really good stories."

Cicero ignored the ferret and turned to Marco. "Please take your friend out of the library. We are already pressing our luck, having meetings in the storeroom, and few are allowed in my chambers. I fear he will get us all kicked out."

Marco hung his head. "Come on Polo. Let's go." He steered the ferret out through the door.

Cicero heard Polo chattering all the way down the hall. "I'm sorry. I didn't mean to get you in trouble. I don't know why he's so grumpy, though. Why *is* he so grumpy, Marco?"

Cicero jumped down from the chair and poked his head out the door. "Marco! After you take him outside, come back in here. I need to talk to you."

Cicero curled up on a chair and put his head down, weighed by the decision he needed to make. He had to be sure.

The room filled with the radiance only Alaniah could make.

"Ahhh, Alaniah. I need your light right now."

"Why so glum, Cicero-ero-o?"

"I am feeling the days," said Cicero.

"There is something more, I think."

"Yes, Alaniah. So long I've been waiting, I'd almost given up. I was too careless before; overlooked too many obvious signs. I fear making a wrong decision again and that's not like me. I've never been a fearful cat."

"This is true."

"I must have no reservations."

"Yes, but you cannot know everything ahead of time. Wherein lies your uncertainty?"

"Marco seems... I don't know... too young." He sighed and closed his eyes.

"Weren't you but a kit when you set foot on this path? Can you not remember your own impetuous youth?"

"It was so many lifetimes ago."

"Then what will you do?"

"I need to look to the Code to see if Marco is up to the challenge. Why do I not remember these things?" said Cicero worriedly. "So first, does he pass the test for courage?"

"Did he not do battle with three others who were much larger?

"Yes, that might be courage. Yet it might be foolishness."

"What is foolishness?"

"I often wonder what the difference is... between courage and foolishness. If we knew what we were getting ourselves into, we probably wouldn't do much but sleep. It takes a bit of madness to jump into the middle of things which might turn out badly. Marco shows a remarkable aptitude for this reckless kind of courage we talk about."

"Isn't that what you're looking for?"

"Yes... and honor, compassion, humility, self-sacrifice. Many things it takes to make a Guardian. Marco did not hesitate to help save Lily when the raccoons had her. That's the kind of thing I mean. He does jump in when things need to happen. He is good that way."

They sat in silence for while, Cicero pondering and Alaniah quietly hovering.

"He's intelligent and I believe he has the other qualities, but I wonder about his judgment," Cicero finally said.

"What do you mean?"

"Well... it's his friendship with that ferret. Why does Marco waste his time with him? Polo is such a foolish and undignified creature."

Alaniah flew up in a swoop and came down to face Cicero. "This is how you measure his wisdom? Dear Cicero, are you not lacking in tolerance? Polo is not an intelligent creature, but he is a pure soul."

"Oh, my dear Alaniah. Am I being too harsh? I don't mean to be, but I must look at everything. How can I know he will have the wisdom to be successful?"

"Wisdom, understanding? Where does it come from, Cicero? Why are you asking me? You know the answer. He will make mistakes, like you. Earthlings seem to learn everything the hard way-ay."

"So true, Alaniah. So true."

"You are forgetting something else."

Cicero looked to her to continue.

"Marco hears. He hears the frequency. He hears the music of the Book and he hears me, something that never happened with Bait."

Cicero nodded. Marco did have all the signs he'd been looking for. Even the one he didn't mention now, but held as a touchstone, the highest criterion he needed to make his final decision... and that was the connection Marco had made with Akeel.

GUARDIAN-IN-TRAINING

Marco knew he was in trouble, but Cicero was being unfair. Like Polo, he wondered why the old cat was in such a foul temper.

Outside Cicero's door, he peeked around the edge and took a quick sniff to test the atmosphere inside.

Cicero spotted him and called out in a spirited voice. "Marco! What took you so long? Come in!"

Marco's eyes widened and he stepped in the room. "I'm... not in trouble?"

"On the contrary!" exclaimed Cicero. "My displeasure was not with you, but due to grave matters at hand. Decisions, calling on clear judgment and needing certitude cause vexation to the spirit."

Marco wondered if Cicero might be apologizing. It was hard to tell.

"Today is a most auspicious day."

"It is?" Marco asked. 'Auspicious' sounded like something to worry about, but Cicero was too light hearted.

"Most assuredly. I will tell you now that these past weeks you have been on trial. Not for any crime committed, but to measure your worthiness. Careful observation and analysis of your actions have revealed crucial characteristics required for this post. Being a Guardian Cat demands a high level of integrity."

Marco had no clue what Cicero was talking about, so he remained silent.

"To put it more simply," Cicero continued, "when you have reached the end of your journey, how will you view it? Will you be able to say you led an honorable life? Or to paraphrase someone, 'I have suffered, it is true, as few men... uh... cats... are ever called upon to suffer, but I have been weighed in the balances by a jury of my peers and found not wanting?'"

As usual, Cicero's long-winded explanations, punctured with quotes, confused Marco even more. Cicero finally noticed his bewilderment.

"Alaniah, would you please convey the nature of this momentous event to our young friend?"

Alaniah floated down from a high corner to join them. "It would be my honor-or," she sang. "Marco, what Cicero is trying to say is that he has chosen you to be his successor."

Marco's breath caught in his throat. Whatever he'd been expecting, it certainly wasn't this. "I don't know what... to say," he stammered.

"You may say yes,'" teased Alaniah. "That would please Cicero most."

"Yes," he consented. Then he repeated it with vigor as the realization sunk in.

"Good. I *am* most pleased." said Cicero. "Let us proceed to the hidden chamber."

Marco followed Cicero downstairs to the mirror, thinking about his dream come true. Even though it came as a surprise, it did seem like his destiny. He was feeling nobler already and could hardly wait to tell someone.

As they waited for Alaniah to open the mirror portal for them, Cicero sat looking forward, "You can't tell anyone!"

Marco jumped. How did Cicero know what he was thinking? It was beginning to spook him. They descended down the dark, dungeon-like stairs once again. This time though, he knew what awaited him at the bottom.

When they reached the door of the underground chamber, Alaniah floated through and disappeared, leaving them in utter darkness. Marco bumped into Cicero.

"Hang on. Sometimes she gets distracted. She also likes to mess with us."

The door opened and the chamber glowed with light swirling in a rainbow of colors. "I prepared the room especially for this occasion. You may enter now," said Alaniah.

Cicero allowed Marco to enter first. He felt a ripple of excitement. When he came here before, he'd been so naïve. Not anymore, he thought.

"Very well, Marco," said Cicero. "We have no time to waste. Please come and sit in front of me."

Marco stepped in closer to Cicero. Cicero raised his paw and placed it on Marco's head. "Marco, as of this moment, you are officially a Guardian-in-training."

Cicero removed his paw and jumped up to the table.

"Is that it?" asked Marco thoughtlessly. In books, ceremonies were always very elaborate, especially for knighthood, which was how he thought of his new position.

"What did you expect?"

"I don't know. Something… more…" Marco felt foolish putting it into words.

"A celestial being who deems to talk to you, a time traveling journey back to the most magnificent library ever created, a meeting with the original human Guardian, witnessing a major historical event and being here in the presence of the most powerful and magical book in existence…" Cicero said sternly. "What more do you want?"

Reduced to a speck of dust, Marco turned his face to wash a non-existent itch on his back. Cicero would change his mind now, probably throwing him out on his ear.

"Marco, look at me. We are cats. Try to remember that," said Cicero simply. "Now come up here and let's have no more foolishness."

Marco looked up at Cicero, who had made his blunder vanish like a puff of smoke. With this cat, nothing was predictable.

Marco jumped quickly up to the table. Alaniah flew in swirls around the room, in ever-smaller circles, until she landed on top of the box. As soon as she touched it, one side of the box opened up like a flower. Inside was Akeel's book.

Marco gasped. "It really is Akeel's book." He looked around the room, half expecting to see him. "I wish he were here."

"I understand. I do feel his presence when I am with the book. This is his legacy, however."

"So... Akeel brought the book here?"

"No, but someday I will tell you the story of how we both came to be in this place."

Marco started feeling cocky again. "Make it do something. Like Akeel did."

"Not allowed."

"What do you mean? You are the Guardian. You can do whatever you want, right?"

"Yes... and no."

"That's not much of an answer. Here I am, on my first day of training. So train me."

He felt Cicero's glare, but he didn't feel like backing off.

Finally Cicero gave in. "I will show you one small thing. But understand this. You cannot use its magic except for very serious matters. Life and death. Or to save the Book itself. Its power is addictive and it becomes dangerous to the one using it."

Marco waited eagerly.

"Marco?"

"Yes?"

"Do you understand?"

Marco was sure the right answer was 'yes'. "Yes, Cicero."

Cicero looked around the barren cave-like room with only a table and the Book.

"Hop down," he ordered Marco.

They both jumped off the table. Cicero closed his eyes and mumbled some words, and the table changed shape. In one smooth transformation, the top became a piece of thick clear-cut glass, and the legs appeared to be growing out of the floor like a tree trunk.

Cicero looked pleased. "I may leave it that way. It's one way I keep in practice… changing the table."

Marco could not believe how lame this trick was. "How will this help me? What if I'm in some life or death situation? I hardly think redecorating tables will save anyone!"

"You want something more dramatic?" Cicero sighed. "Okay, Marco, just this once I will give you dramatic. You will need to learn the language anyway." Cicero closed his eyes. "I usually say this silently." He began to chant in a strange language.

"Fa-taw-lah-nee, rah-ma-la-nee, ma-fa-taw-nee, moon-too-lah."

Marco had never heard anything so silly in his life. He yawned—and because his eyes were closed for a half second—he missed how the magic happened. When he opened them, a strange human towered above him.

Spooked, Marco turned and ran out the door, but he stopped on the other side to peer back inside. The man was chuckling and holding out his hand to Marco. "Is this dramatic enough?"

"Cicero?"

The man looked at Marco and smiled. "Yes?"

"You're human?"

Cicero as a man reached down to pick up Marco and scratch behind his ears. "I always wanted to see what that felt like to a human."

Marco loved being held again. "Will you stay like this?" he purred.

"Oh my, no," replied Cicero. "Being human is much too complicated."

LIBRARY INVADERS

Sting never hated cats before. He never even thought about them except when they got in his way. What was he doing wasting his precious time stalking this stupid Marco? Hanging out by the library, for pete's sake. But there he was, climbing a tree with that ridiculous ferret right behind him.

But at least he knew he was in the right place. The strange raccoon had been telling the truth about the cats' new hideout. He didn't know what to think about Lazer. He'd never taken advice from anyone before, so why was he listening to this guy?

Oh yeah, something about the cats having magical powers because of a book. And if he was right about the cats, then he must be right about the warehouse full of food. Sting's mouth watered at the thought of so much food all in one place. More than he could eat, Lazer told him. Hah! Like that was possible.

"Crimmany, go see what he's up to," he ordered. "Maybe he's got the book in there."

Crimmany dutifully climbed up the tree and looked in the library window.

"Well? What's in there?" Sting whispered loudly.

"Not much."

"What are they doing? Readin'?" Sting yelled sarcastically, not bothering anymore to keep quiet.

"Mostly sleeping."

"Stupid cats," Sting muttered. "Well, if they're sleeping it oughta be easy. All we got to do is steal the book and we're home free."

"Home free? Whaddya mean, boss?"

Sting couldn't explain it to these two morons, but he couldn't exactly remember what Lazer had said either, and it didn't make quite as much sense now. Oh well, they'd be eatin' good. That was the most important thing.

"We steal their book and we'll be smarter and stronger."

"You told us we already were smarter and stronger," whined Crimmany.

"Of course we are!" snapped Sting. "But if we have their book, the cats will go back to being normal—like stupid alley cats. That's obvious, isn't it? Enough talk. It's time for action."

Besides being the meanest, one of the reasons Sting was the leader was his scouting abilities, and this time, too, he was able to find a tunnel that got them inside the library. The raccoons clambered over each other, trying to be the first one through. Sting won, of course. Crimmany came next, but was too slow and Tank kicked him in the backside.

Once inside, they stopped in their tracks, awestruck. They were immersed in a sea of books.

Sting was almost reverent. "This is gonna be a bigger job than I thought," he said. For a moment, he was overcome by the atmosphere, by things he didn't have the brain cells or language to explain.

Then he came to his senses. "Figures cats'd hang out in a place like this."

"Disgustin' ain't it?" Tank said.

Crimmany piped up, "Hey, maybe we should learn to read." He spotted a table with children's books lying out. "I'll bet it's not that hard." He climbed on the table and opened one. "Oh, cool pictures. Take a look, you guys."

Tank started to wander over, but Sting nudged him, rolling his eyes and staring at the ceiling.

"It might be kinda fun. We should give it a try," insisted Crimmany.

"Why would I want to read?" barked Sting. "If I want to know somethin' I'll ask a cat!" He wadded up a piece of newspaper and threw it at Crimmany.

"Cut it out!" yelled Crimmany, abandoning the book. He made his own paper wad and ran after Sting. In the midst of the tussle, Sting caught a movement from the second floor balcony.

He froze, even as one of Crimmany's paper balls struck him on the head. How long had that stupid cat been spying on him? He cursed under his breath.

"Well, look who's here!" Sting said to Marco, as if he didn't absolutely loathe him. "I believe we've met before. Let's see, you're the Defender of Deformed Rats, aren't you? What are you defending tonight? Must be books, 'cause that's all I see here."

PANDEMONIUM

Marco glared down at Sting from between the rails of the balcony. Why did this creep keep showing up everywhere? Especially here, his refuge from the world. "What are you doing in the library? You can't read."

"You sayin' we're not welcome?"

"That's exactly what I'm saying. Scram."

"Oh, you're hurting my feelings. Hey Marco, why don't you give us a tour? We'd like to improve our minds too. Right, boys?" Sting snickered and looked to the other raccoons.

"Sure thing, Sting."

"See? They like it here. Come on down and join us." Sting walked over to some books and started pawing through them. He picked one out at random. *The Care and Feeding of Orphaned Kittens.* He threw it on the floor.

Marco was at a loss for what to do. Up until now, his encounters with Sting were more like wrestling matches.

"You deaf or something? Maybe you think you're too good for the likes of us," said Sting. "Or maybe... "

Marco could tell Sting thought he was brilliant by the way he strutted about.

"Maybe, you're hidin' something," accused Sting.

Marco's tail bristled as he prepared himself for another clash with the raccoon, but this time the enemy was on his territory. Now that he had been made a Guardian Cat, he would defend not only *The Book of Motion*. He would defend all the books!

Scuffling noises from a far corner of the first floor interrupted Marco's concentration.

"Hey, Marco, there's a whole stash of granola bars in the desk. Nuts, dried fruit, chocolate." It was Polo "And raisins, my favorite!" Polo started towards the bottom of the stairs, holding a crumbling piece of granola bar in his paw. "Want some?" Polo offered generously. Marco had explained more than once that he didn't eat sweets, but Polo never remembered.

Then the small ferret spotted Sting. "Uh-oh," he said.

Sting sauntered towards Polo—casually, like they were friends. "Well, well. Look who else is here."

Marco yelled, "Polo! Run!"

Sting grabbed the ferret. "Ha! I'm not lettin' you go this time!"

Marco had already started down the stairs.

"I see you decided to join me," said Sting.

"Join you? That's a laugh," said Marco.

"Well, at least I know how to laugh. Ain't never seen a cat laugh."

"Cats have a sense of humor," said Marco, moving down each step slowly but deliberately. "But it has to be funny."

Polo squealed.

"Quiet," Sting said, shaking Polo by his neck. "Or I'll make it tighter."

Marco glared at Sting. "*That* is not funny."

"Oh, you're making me cry," said Sting, mocking him. "You want him back? I'll cut you a deal."

"A deal? What are you talking about?"

"We'll trade."

"Trade? Trade what?"

"The Magic Book. Hand it over and you can have your mangy friend back."

Marco's breath caught in his throat and he stopped dead on the stairs. The magic book? How would a disreputable character like Sting know anything about *The Book of Motion*? He *couldn't* be talking about that.

Sting stood in the center of the vestibule under the dome, dangling Polo in the air. "Hey! Where's the rest of your book club? Maybe they know something you don't. Maybe..." Sting paused dramatically. "Just maybe they haven't told you about the book."

Marco's head swirled with questions, but he managed to keep calm. "There's all kinds of books here, Sting. There's even a whole section on magic. Why don't you get a library card and check one out?"

"Ha! I knew it. You don't even know about the book. You don't know nuthin'!"

Marco tasted something bitter in his mouth as he felt a fierceness rising in him. He reached the bottom of the stairs.

"Some friends. Looks to me like you've been deserted, little buddy."

Marco lunged towards his adversary. At the same moment Sting shifted Polo between them, using him as a shield. Marco's claws punctured Polo's skin and he smelled his blood. Polo squealed louder.

"You should take better care of the one friend you got," taunted Sting. "Looks like this little rat is all mine now."

Marco made a second attempt to attack Sting, but everything went black. He took the blow from Tank in his soft underbelly and when he caught his breath, it was filled with the heavy odor of raccoon.

He heard Polo's cry pierce the air again, and just as suddenly, it was squelched. He squirmed out from under Tank and caught sight of Sting shoving Polo down an open grate in the floorboards, then disappearing down the hole after him. Crimmany was lunging forward, ready to attack.

He tried to block himself from Crimmany's next move and failed. Not because of his own moves, but because Tweezer, one of the Dead Cats, appeared out of nowhere in a flying leap, colliding with Crimmany and knocking him to the floor.

Tank sprang to attack and Marco met him in a mid-air collision. All four animals were sprawled on the library floor, books scattered everywhere around them. But the impact broke the momentum of the battle as everybody disentangled themselves and jockeyed to an upright position.

The raccoons ambled off, shoving each other and complaining about who was to blame.

Raccoons have no dignity, Marco thought. Then he turned to Tweezer. "Thanks for covering my back."

"A SHAPE THAT MEANS DECEIT…"

Marco bolted up the stairs, nearly skidding on the landing as he made the turn. He dashed straight into Cicero's chambers without thinking, but something about the old cat stopped him cold. A large volume of Shakespeare was spread out in front of him. His eyes were half closed, but he was anything but sleeping.

"Cicero," started Marco, but Cicero sat as still as a stone cat.

Marco thought Cicero should know what was going on, but when he opened his eyes all he got was a grim look.

"Sorry to disturb you Cicero, but I need to tell you… " How was he going to explain? "We have a problem."

"Really," answered Cicero, his voice flat.

"Sting was here." Marco's mouth was dry and he suddenly felt more afraid of Cicero than he'd been of Sting. "You know, the raccoon."

"I know who Sting is."

Marco plowed ahead with his explanation. "He acts like he knows something about the Book, but he couldn't possibly know. And he's kidnapped Polo. What should we do?"

"What do *you* think we should do?"

"I… I don't know. That's why I'm asking you."

"I saw the whole thing."

"Wha…? What do you mean? You saw Sting?"

"I watched from the balcony."

Marco was confused by Cicero's odd behavior. "Shouldn't we do something? At least, we need to rescue Polo."

Suddenly Cicero was up on all fours, standing on the edge of the table, hunched over and looking down on Marco. For a brief moment, Cicero reminded Marco of a vulture.

"Who did you tell?" demanded Cicero in a roar.

Marco froze. He'd never seen him so angry.

"Did you tell that ridiculous ferret?"

"No, I mean… what do you mean? Tell him what?"

"How would a filthy animal like Sting know anything about the Book?"

Marco wondered the same thing. He also wondered why Cicero was accusing him.

Someone cleared his throat at the door. It was Bait.

"May I enter?" he asked politely. "Or is this a private meeting?"

Marco was relieved to see a friendly face.

"I heard what happened, and I'm here to offer my services," said Bait.

"What services would I need from you?" replied Cicero coldly.

"Come on, Cicero... you *will* need me. The raccoons are onto the Book and you will need an extra hand or two protecting it from those thieves."

Marco thought Bait's proposal seemed generous and didn't understand why Cicero had his back arched. He was also surprised that other cats knew about the Book.

Bait seemed calm, considering Cicero's threatening position. "I'll bet Marco would help, too. Wouldn't you, Marco?"

"Sure. Yeah," said Marco, agreeably.

"See, Cicero. You don't have to do this alone. You do have friends."

Cicero backed off and sat down. He closed his eyes. Bait threw a sideways glance at Marco, as if to indicate how eccentric Cicero was.

Cicero walked the length of the table, as though he were preparing for a speech. Then he spoke in his best Shakespearean.

"Seems he a dove? His feathers are but borrowed for he's disposed as the hateful raven. Is he a lamb? His skin is surely lent him for he's included as is the ravenous wolf. Who cannot steal a shape that means deceit?"

Bait had climbed up on a chair, as if he needed to be on the same level as Cicero. "You foolish old cat! You think quoting Shakespeare solves anything?" Then he jumped to the floor and prepared to leave. "Don't say I didn't warn you. Or offer to help." As he turned to leave, he said to Marco. "Come on, let's leave this burned-out candle."

Marco was torn. Reluctantly he left with Bait, leaving Cicero alone in his chambers.

Bait waited until they were outside to speak. "I fear his reach has exceeded his grasp. He has outlived his usefulness here. He has outlived his job."

"What job?" asked Marco, trying to figure out just what Bait knew about the Book without giving away what he knew. Maybe he was only referring to his job as the library cat, but Marco was getting anxious that too many others knew about the Book, which was supposed to be top secret.

"You know it's all a fairy story, don't you?"

Marco hesitated. Bait made it seem like no big deal. But Marco had made a promise and he had to keep his word. Cicero was acting strangely and sometimes he scared Marco with his passion. But he'd been entrusted to something important and it felt real to him. Marco paused, unsure of what to say.

"I'll bet he made you promise not to tell, didn't he? That's just part of his mental illness." Bait shook his head. "But don't worry about him. You've got other problems, Marco."

ERRORS IN JUDGMENT

Cicero had misjudged Marco. He was thankful for that. Whatever trouble was brewing with the raccoons, he felt sure Bait was behind it after that little counterfeit display of friendship. It made sense, considering what had happened. But what truly disturbed him was the fact that he had misjudged Bait. Again.

He had chosen Bait to be his successor years ago, but had to let him go. Now he was beginning to realize how much he'd underestimated Bait's resentment for that.

At the time, Cicero had no choice. The incident with Caffeina was disturbing especially because Bait thought no one was listening. A Guardian always treated a lady with respect and Bait had accused Caffeina of being a tramp. It was important that a Guardian have the same good character when alone, as well as when others were around.

Bait had seemed surprised about the reprimand, contrite even. It wasn't serious enough to terminate his training, but Cicero's eyes were opened and he kept a close watch.

Things came to a head, though, when Bait questioned him about using the power of the Book. He'd started off politely, appearing to be casual about it. Cicero explained to Bait about abusing the responsibility. A Guardian is rarely called upon to use the power. His only job is to protect it.

Bait claimed that he would only use its power for good. After his arguments didn't work on Cicero, his tone changed, and for the briefest flash, Cicero saw Bait's polished exterior crack. In that moment, Cicero saw the darkness underneath.

What a dreadful feeling that had been. He'd felt like a fool not seeing it before, but Bait's deception had been flawless. Or had it? Did he miss crucial signs? Bait had seemed to be the most qualified cat to come along in years. He presented a noble character and was not afraid of danger. Now Cicero realized his dignified appearance was more a characteristic of his breed, rather than a personal quality.

Cicero had been shocked then. Now he was mortified. How could it have happened again? He cringed at the thought of how close Bait had come to being in the position of a Guardian Cat.

Cicero had given Bait a stern warning and told him his training was finished. Maybe he'd been too harsh. Maybe he should have been more diplomatic, but he'd reacted with passion, and there was no going back.

Bait hung around, came to meetings and nothing changed much on the outside. Cicero did not discourage him from coming. In fact, he thought it was better to keep him close. No one else knew what had happened, but then no one else knew about the Book.

Now Bait was befriending Marco. Nothing good could come of it, he was sure. It also seemed that he was trying to get the raccoons to do his dirty work. What in the world was Bait up to?

SPYING ON CATS

Lazer, the renegade raccoon who had befriended Sting, stood outside the raccoons' camper and toyed with the leash around the sleeping ferret's neck. He was pleased to see Sting had captured him. Pleased to know just how far the raccoon would go.

He banged on Sting's door. Crimmany opened it and stuck his head out. "What do you want?"

"Sting here?" asked Lazer.

"Yeah. So?"

"So! Let me talk to him," barked Lazer.

"Sting!" yelled Crimmany, back inside the camper.

"What!"

"Somebody's here to see you."

Sting appeared as a silhouette, filling the frame of the door. "Hey, Lazer!"

"Hey. How's it going, Sting?"

"Not so good. Come on in."

Lazer climbed into the camper shell and made himself comfortable on shreds of what had been a mattress. "What happened?"

"You never told me the library was full of books! Then that mangy orange cat who keeps buttin' his head in my business showed up. *And* that useless critter I got tied up outside. What am I? A pet sitter? Dang animal sure is a pack of trouble. Only thing he might be good for is some kind of bribe."

"I like the way you think, Sting."

Sting shook his head. "Well, I sure never got that book you was talking about. It's like looking for a needle in a haystack."

"Hmmm. Well, you did one good thing. The cats are all riled up."

"Yeah, that's always a good thing," said Sting. "By the way, where you been?"

"I work undercover, like I told you. Spying on cats."

"Yeah? Seems like a boring job. What for?"

"I have my reasons," said Lazer. "One thing I do know... the cats are worried that you'll steal their big-deal book. They are trying to figure out what to do with it. That means they're likely to move it somewhere." It was a lie, but Lazer had no problem with lying.

"Yeah. So."

"If we can catch them in the act, it'll be a piece of cake."

"We? What's with this 'we' business? Why should I bother?" asked Sting.

"You like having these scruffy strays in your face all the time? Can't you see there's something wrong with them? These cats are not normal."

"You're telling me."

"It's their magical powers. They get it from this book, I tell you. Get it away from them, and you won't have any more problems."

"Why don't *you* deal with them? Why are you asking me?"

Lazer hung his head. "Take a good look at me. I was the runt in my family. They didn't even expect me to live. I've got a good head, but physically... you tell me. You think I could handle these cats?"

"You have a point."

"I need someone like you and your crew. Tough guys."

Sting lit up. "We can handle 'em for sure. Right, boys?"

"Right!" agreed Tank and Crimmany.

Sting paced the length of his truck bed, his center of operations. The other raccoons kept still while he plotted. After a good while, he stopped thinking and gave an order.

"Crimmany, front and center," he said. "I need you to deliver a message."

What magic book?

By now all the Dead Cats had heard about the fight and Polo's kidnapping. They were in their own headquarters in the library storage room and Tweezer was recounting the details, as he knew them, for the umpteenth time.

"What's Sting want a book for?" asked one of the cats.

"There's a jillion books here. Why doesn't he just take one?" asked another.

Marco sat sullenly on top of a card catalogue. Cats could listen to the same story over and over again and never tire of it, but he was growing impatient. This was getting them no closer to rescuing Polo or protecting the Book. He washed his face and listened. The Dead Cats' conversation revealed one important point, and that was how little they really knew about anything.

He had his own set of questions. How could Cicero believe he'd betrayed him? How did Sting know about the Book? And how much did Bait really know?

There was movement outside and a head appeared in the window. The raccoon looked nervously around the room. "Which one of you's Marco?" he demanded.

Marco stood up in surprise.

"This message is for you." The raccoon cleared his throat and spoke like he was repeating the words from memory. "Deliver the magic book to me, I mean Sting, in one hour." His head disappeared and popped back up. "Bring it to him at his headquarters."

He disappeared again. Tweezer was rushing over to look out the window when the raccoon popped up for the third time. "If you don't show, your little buddy's dead meat."

Now all of the cats ran over to the window, crowding each other for a view of the raccoon as he clumsily clawed his way down the tree.

They all began talking at once, but everyone was pretty much saying the same thing.

"Magic book? What magic book?"

Marco slipped out unnoticed.

NEITHER CAT NOR HUMAN

Marco had no problem locating Sting's headquarters. It wouldn't have taken his exceptional sense of smell to detect raccoon odor radiating from the brown truck. Besides, there was Polo, tied to the bumper. Even asleep he looked forlorn.

He must have sensed Marco's presence because he woke up, squealing with delight, and began running towards him. But the leash caught him short.

Sting came out of the camper to see what the commotion was about. "Knock it off!" he yelled and yanked on the leash, choking Polo as he pulled him back. Then he noticed Marco. "Hey, Rat! Look who's here! It's your big buddy."

"Let him go!" demanded Marco.

"Sure, Marco. No problem. But I don't see no book. You didn't come all the way out here without it, did you?"

"It's not mine to give you, Sting."

"I don't care whose it is. Steal it!"

"What are *you* going to do with a book? You can't even read."

"I hear this one's special. Maybe I won't have to read it. Maybe it will read itself to me."

If Marco had any doubts about a traitor in his midst, they were dispelled now. Even if he didn't have his facts straight, there was no way Sting would know about *The Book of Motion* by himself. His head hung down, weighted by a muddle of problems. How had his life gotten so complicated?

"What a moron. I don't know why I'm bothering with the likes of you. Here I thought you'd do anything to get your friend back," said Sting. "Time to proceed with Plan B." Sting yelled back inside the camper, "You boys know what to do. Now go!"

Tank squeezed through the door, Sting not bothering to move to let him out.

"I'm calling in backup," he told Marco. "Friends who are itchin' for a good fight."

"I'm not afraid," Marco countered. "Cats love a good fight."

"You'll be sorry you didn't make this nice and simple, Marco. Be prepared for things to get rough." Sting looked at Polo, "Right, little buddy?"

Polo was shivering, his eyes pleading for mercy.

Marco needed some leverage. Something besides another attack. He'd already been in too many fights with Sting. He would have to go about this differently, and he'd already given some thought to it. A guardian was allowed to use the power of the Book if it was a matter of life and death. Surely, this was one of those times.

He had memorized the magical words. Cicero said he wasn't ready to receive the spell, but their haunting sound had stayed with him. So he spoke the words, hoping to transform into a human like Cicero had done. Nothing happened at first. Marco repeated the spell. Again nothing. What was he doing wrong? He tried a third time and was suddenly catapulted into a new form. He was the same size as before and still on all fours, but he had the arms and legs of a human. They were covered in fur, but his face felt naked and his ears were gone.

He was neither cat nor human, but a frightful hodgepodge of both. Sting and Polo were both gaping at him. When Sting started laughing, Marco, mortified at his condition, ran for cover, tripping and falling, forced to use legs that didn't fit his body.

CAFFEINA

Marco returned to the library in a strange mood, smelling of human and raccoon, warning the Dead Cats of impending danger. When someone asked him what was wrong, he snapped at them. But he'd taken charge and was giving orders. They needed lookouts because the raccoons were bringing in recruits for a fight. Marco said they needed their own recruits, that they needed to round up some strays.

The air was charged with electricity and Caffeina chose to join the round up rather than sit around waiting. It turned out that only she and Tweezer had volunteered.

"How much farther?" whined Caffeina, after they been walking forever. She thought it might be fun going on an adventure, but she should have known better. How could anything be fun with Tweezer?

Now she wished she'd stayed behind, because her toe pads hurt.

"Tweezer! You never told me it would be this far. For that matter, you never even told me where we're going."

Tweezer did not slow his pace or miss a beat.

"We've no time to waste, Caffeina."

"I know. It's just that I figured stray cats would be... well, like, closer to town."

"You don't get out much, do you?"

"You are such a pain, Tweezer! Why are you so mean?"

"I'm not mean. I just don't have time to explain things."

After a few blocks he slowed his pace. "We're almost there." They turned the corner and Tweezer crossed the street in front of a dilapidated old house. The yard was surrounded by a chain link fence, and the house was wrapped with a wide porch supported by thick pillars covered in dry paint curls.

It looked abandoned, but there were cats dozing on chairs and in laundry baskets. Kittens scrambled around the dirt yard, playing with broken twigs. Aluminum pie tins of dry food lined the porch.

For once, Caffeina was speechless. She had no idea so many cats could live in one place. Tweezer climbed up the trunk of a tree and leaped off inside the fenced yard. He marched up to the porch like he belonged.

"Welcome home, Tweez. How's it going?"

This was where Tweezer lived? Caffeina never thought about where the other cats went when they weren't together. She'd always been a little ashamed because she lied about living at the Sleep N'Go. She picked her way around mud puddles and tried not to breathe too deeply. This was so much worse than the motel.

She joined Tweezer so she wouldn't get stuck out in the yard having to talk with some awful-looking stray.

"Tweezer! Where you been? Hanging out with bookworms?" yelled one dirty white cat.

"They're dead cats, supposedly," said another.

"Aren't we good enough for you anymore?"

"Maybe we're not dead enough," joked one.

To Caffeina's surprise, Tweezer didn't get uptight with these cats like he did with her. He greeted each one like they were long lost brothers and sisters, all of them teasing each other good-naturedly.

"Look what he brought with him! Hey, gorgeous. What's your name?"

"Wow, Tweezer. How'd you ever get a girl like that? You being so ugly and all."

Caffeina was appalled they thought she was Tweezer's girl.

"Naw, she's just a friend," said Tweezer.

"Sure. We believe that."

"Hey, Tweez! If she's not your girl, maybe I can have her," said Boris, an obese orange and white cat. "What about it, baby?"

"No way, creep." Caffeina said. She was not used to such crudeness. The Dead Cats, except for Bait, were always respectful.

"Aw, you're hurtin' my feelings!" said Boris. "I need a pretty girl to talk to."

"Okay, come here. I do have something to say," said Caffeina.

Boris came waddling over with a stupid grin on his face, and the minute he was close enough, Caffeina smacked him a good one, drawing a thin line of blood on his nose.

"Geez, you don't have to get violent," said Boris, dragging his tail as he walked away.

Meanwhile, Tweezer had jumped onto a table. "Alright. Listen up, everybody. I came here for a reason and I don't have a lot of time for explanations, so I'll get right to the point. We need your help."

"We? Like who's 'we'?"

"The Dead Cats Society. We've been attacked by a pack of raccoons. They're roaming through town, looking for trouble, and…"

"Raccoons! Those mangy varmints," interrupted a cat.

"What's a raccoon?" asked a kitten.

"But…" continued Tweezer, holding up his paw. "This pack is particularly vicious and they've called for more recruits. The rumors are flying, but if they're true we won't stand a chance."

"What'd you do to get them so riled up, Tweezer?"

"It's kinda complicated, but they've kidnapped one of our friends and are holding him hostage."

"Kidnapped! Who'd kidnap a cat? I thought everyone wanted to get rid of us."

"Um, well," Tweezer faltered. "Polo's not exactly a cat."

"What exactly is he?" said one.

Tweezer looked to Caffeina for help. She shrugged. "Might as well tell them the truth," she said.

"It's a ferret," said Tweezer.

"A what?"

"He's a parrot?" inquired a half-deaf, half-tailed Manx. "Ruby's been looking kinda' lonely lately."

Tweezer's look was one Caffeina had never seen before. Sort of a helpless, exasperated expression, but this time he was not annoyed with her. He took a deep breath and explained to her, like he was taking her into his confidence. "Ruby is a parrot, a long time resident here at Mrs. Wilcox's."

To the others, he said, "No, not a parrot. A ferret."

There was dead silence until a kitten piped up and asked, "What's a ferret?"

Again, Tweezer appealed to Caffeina. "Can you help me out here?"

The strays were waiting.

She sighed. "Well, he looks a little like us, but he's long and has small ears." That wasn't much help. Then she remembered how Marco had described him. "Oh, yeah. He's funny."

"Ooooh," the cats all breathed out simultaneously, as if it explained everything.

"So I'm asking for your help," Tweezer went on. "How about an adventure?"

The cats stared at him in utter astonishment.

Tweezer plowed on. "What are you doing here? You don't have to hunt for food. You've all gone soft. Come on and live a little. Break out of your routine."

Caffeina thought Tweezer was overselling the mission, but she admired the spirit of his speech.

But the cats weren't buying it.

"Adventure? Why in the world would we want an adventure? We like eating and sleeping and we love being spoiled by our human," said one.

"Yeah, why would we risk our necks to fight wild raccoons? That's not an adventure. That's suicide!" said another.

Tweezer pleaded with them, which was something he wasn't used to doing. "What if you were in trouble? Wouldn't you want someone to come and rescue you?"

"Tweezer. Look around. In case you forgot, we've already been rescued."

Tweezer didn't respond, and Caffeina worried he'd run out of arguments. Before she even realized what she was doing, she jumped onto the table next to him. "You don't realize how serious this is. These raccoons are not only out for our blood, but you may well be their next victims. And then you'll be begging for our help."

"Well, well. The little princess has spoken," said Lulu, an old female, who was not aging gracefully. "You're scaring us, Princess."

Contrary to her normal behavior, Caffeina ignored her. She'd deal with this female later. Besides, she was beginning to enjoy delivering this little pep talk.

"There's more at stake here than defense and rescue. They're planning a heist."

Tweezer leaned over close to her. "You have to use simpler words," he whispered.

"Oh, sure. Uh, a heist is like a burglary." She looked at Tweezer and he motioned to go down a notch.

"Stealing."

"Yeah, what can they steal from a cat?"

She knew it was going to sound strange, but what could she do? "A book. From the library."

"What's a library?" asked the kitten.

"Oh, my. That does sound serious," said Lulu. "You Dead Cats are so weird. The rumors are true."

"Why would we care about some stupid book?" yelled Boris, the dirty white fat cat.

This was not going well. Caffeina thought quickly and decided to take a different approach. Even though she'd never read much more than fashion magazines, she had absorbed Cicero's teachings. She had listened to his tales about the Guardian Cats, their gallant and noble deeds and now, when she needed them, they came to her rescue. Just knowing about them inspired her.

"Think about others for a change. Don't be concerned only with your own lot. Test your courage and strength." She paused and took a deep breath. "See what you're made of. You won't know until you've put it to the test."

She looked into their faces. "Think of it as a quest," she said a little breathlessly.

Caffeina felt Tweezer staring in amazement at her.

"What's a quest?" asked a kitten.

WHEN RUMORS ARE NOT ENOUGH

Bait was on the library roof. He felt the charge in the air. Tonight was the night. Tonight he would get his revenge.

He never thought that treating a 'girl' badly would put him out of the league of Guardians. Then of course, there was that time he let his shield down. That fraction of a second had cost him dearly, but it was Cicero who would pay. His old mentor, who had taken him in and given him the attention he'd never received.

It was all he ever wanted, and when he first met Cicero, all that had changed. The old cat took him everywhere. They would sit for hours together in the chambers, and Bait would listen to the Guardian stories and countless other stories of adventure and intrigue. They went out at night, stalking and hunting. He told Cicero about his own past, his shows, his awards. Finally, he told him about being dumped by his human.

Then Cicero abandoned him. Just like that, it was all over. Bait kept up his appearances. That was the one thing he excelled at. But inwardly, he seethed with resentment. He vowed that, whatever it took, he would steal the thing that mattered most to Cicero.

He was not in a hurry, and he took up reading books on magic. He discovered he had a gift for it.

At first, he learned how to change his appearance in small ways. His fur color, his eyes. Then he concentrated on more radical alterations until he was able to completely disguise himself. It was then that he realized the intense attraction he had toward Cicero's Book. More than revenge, Bait wanted the Book for himself.

A shadow moving on the roof crept over and sat next to Bait.

"You make a good raccoon," said the Whisperer.

"I know. An opposable thumb makes everything possible," Bait said. He felt himself starting to shake. He could almost taste the power of magic, as if it were a drug. Black magic. It was so delicious.

Now when he needed its power the most, something was wrong.

"I can't hold the shapes as long," he told the shadow.

"You must get your power from the Book now. It is the only power that will serve one so advanced as you."

"I'm working on it!" flared Bait, but he felt himself growing weaker.

He could almost feel the vibration that came right before he brought about a transformation. Enough to make him crave it all the more, but when his power was too weak, it made his craving stronger.

"You must control yourself," breathed the Whisperer.

"Yes. You are right," said Bait. He tried to calm himself. "Tonight I will know if my plan will work. If Cicero is worried about the safety of the Book, he will try to move it. In all this time, I have not been allowed to get close to it. Tonight, though, you will see something amazing. It is sure to frighten Cicero into action."

"What about the raccoons? Are they helping you?"

"They are too stupid to carry this off. They don't care about the Book, but they do have a personal vendetta against the cats. They kidnapped that stupid ferret—for what, I don't know. It's okay. I only needed them to create a diversion, and that's exactly what they did."

"I told you that rumors were the best tool, didn't I?" whispered the formless one.

"Yes, but it's not enough to get Cicero to move the Book. It has to be more threatening."

"You have something in mind?"

"Most definitely, but I need to rest. I need all of my strength to transform later."

"I have things to attend to as well," said the Whisperer. "Don't fail. There's too much at stake, and if you aren't successful... I will have to report back to my benefactor. Be sure we have something good to tell him."

POWER IN THE WRONG HANDS

The Dead Cats positioned themselves in the magnolia tree, waiting to ambush the raccoons. They were bored.

A large beetle crawled along a branch. Tweezer pounced and gobbled it up in one move.

"Eeew!" said Caffeina. "How can you eat those things?"

"I'm hungry," said Tweezer.

"Well, so am I, but I draw the line at cockroaches."

"They have lots of protein. You could probably use some protein."

"What I *need* is a visit to a salon. White fur is such a pain."

Tweezer peered at her through his one good eye. "Ahhh. You don't look so bad," he said.

Marco was deep in thought on a branch above the others. He was glad Cicero hadn't found out about him trying to use the spell, but he still cringed when he thought about the strange creature he'd become. That whole night he'd hidden in a tree, terrified that he'd never be normal again.

Now he had other things to worry about. The cats, as usual, had no plan, and Tweezer said they had no luck rounding up recruits. They needed a miracle.

"Hey, Marco! You sure tonight's the night? We've been up here forever."

"Be patient, Skitzo."

From far off came the soft deep rumble of thunder. Out of the corner of his eye, Marco caught some movement in the bushes. A small raccoon moved in and out of the shadows, then darted across an open space toward the library. Was this one of Sting's gang?

The other cats were too absorbed in small talk to notice, so when the raccoon climbed into a basement window opening, Marco went to investigate.

He slipped through the upper story window and made his way to the balcony, where he scanned the lower floor through the rails. The raccoon soon appeared, his head poking through the same floor vent Sting had used.

But this was not Sting. He was way too small. The raccoon moved to a table with newspapers and magazines and promptly went to work ripping them into shreds, being careful to keep them in a pile. Strange, but hardly threatening. If this was the raccoons' big move, then he didn't have much to worry about.

The raccoon was fumbling with something in his paws. There was a soft scraping sound, a familiar odor and an orange spark. "Stupid thing," the animal mumbled. "What's the matter with it?"

Marco sat, spellbound, observing from his catwalk, as though the scene below were a theater stage. A clattering noise echoed in the darkened library. The raccoon had dropped the object.

He used both paws to pick it up again. A flicker of sparks sprayed out. "Dang!" The odor grew stronger and Marco realized what it was—Polo's cigarette lighter! How in the world did this raccoon get it? He had to be a friend of Sting's.

The raccoon's next attempt was successful. The flame, framed by an orange halo, burned steadily. The raccoon moved the lighter close to the torn pile of newspaper, which took the flame, turning it yellow and blue. It flared up into the raccoons face, singeing his whiskers.

"Cripes!" he shouted. Then the fire steadied and the raccoon mumbled to himself. "I always say, if you want something done right, do it yourself." He turned and gazed into the depths of the library and Marco got a better view of his face. He wondered if his eyes were playing tricks on him.

The raccoon's face started to change shape. No, it was more like there were two faces. Marco blinked and tried to refocus his eyes. Now it was more visible, the raccoon and another animal forming within the raccoon. It was not possible, what he was seeing. But it was happening. There was another creature coming to life, another body inside the raccoon.

What kind of magic was at work? Nothing seemed to be as it appeared on the surface anymore. He felt dizzy for a moment and thought of *The Book of Motion* and how Akeel and Cicero had tried to explain about power in the wrong hands. He thought about his own error in judgment, trying to use power he wasn't ready for.

"No!" The raccoon shouted. "Don't leave me now!"

The fire grew larger, but the paper burned out quickly, and so the flames died down to almost nothing. The raccoon frantically tore up more paper, throwing it onto the hot ashes. He tried manipulating the lighter again, but it was getting harder for him to manage.

The raccoon was getting worked up, struggling with the creature that appeared to be taking over his body. The small fire smoldered and the morphing creature became more fluid as it grew angrier. It, or they, Marco couldn't tell which one, threw the whole lighter onto the fire.

The double creature seemed to waiver back and forth, from what it was, to whatever it was becoming. The second creature had dull gray fur and no stripes. The lighter exploded and the fire leaped into action.

The transformation was complete. The creature within the creature had prevailed. Marco was looking at one of the Dead Cats.

GATHERING SMOKE

Cicero heard a small explosion, but it was the smell of smoke that alarmed him. He dashed out of his chambers towards the balcony. He stared at the flames, not believing his eyes, thinking this must be a nightmare and he would surely wake up. When smoke drifted upwards, he knew this was no dream.

Fire was Cicero's greatest fear... his only fear, ever since he'd witnessed the burning of Alexandria. He stared at it in a daze. He knew he should move, but he remained petrified, dreading to leave as though he could will the fire to stop by his being there.

"What dark power has come upon me... that I should suffer through this, as did my predecessors? And why did I not sense its coming?"

Finally, he turned and darted back to his chambers, looking for Alaniah. She was not there and he went back to the balcony, coughing on the gathering smoke.

Cicero stood in front of the mirror, helpless to enter without Alaniah. He saw the reflection of the fire behind him, the image repeating over and over because of another mirror on the other side. For a terrifying moment, he felt the presence of the madmen who burned the library at Alexandria.

CAFFEINA GOES FOR HELP

"**D**id you hear that noise? And what is that smell?" Caffeina caught the scent first, then Tweezer and the others smelled it.

"It's coming from inside!" cried Skitzo.

Gypsy leaped down onto a lower branch. "Fire!" she cried. "I can see it. Come over here and look."

"Fire?" cried Skitzo. "This is how they've come to destroy us?"

"They? Who do you mean? The raccoons?" asked Caffeina.

"We need a human," said Gypsy, ever the practical one. "They'll know what to do."

"Where are we going to find a human at this time of night?"

"There's a light on in that house," said Pudge. "Who's willing to check it out?"

"I'll go," said Caffeina. "I can't sit here and do nothing."

She dropped down from the tree and ran to the house. The rose bushes pricked her nose as she climbed up the trellis, but she managed to get to the window and peer inside where two people were sitting in front of a TV.

Caffeina tapped on the window with her paw. They didn't hear her. She tapped harder and louder. This time the woman turned and looked out the window. She squinted at her and laughed, then nudged her husband. He ignored her. She nudged him again.

Caffeina caught a whiff of smoke and tapped more vigorously. The woman was laughing now, but the man was getting annoyed.

Caffeina meowed at the humans, hoping that they would come outside and smell the smoke. The man groaned as he got out of his chair and came over to the window.

'Oh good,' thought Caffeina hopefully. 'They'll be sure to help us now.'

"Damn stray cat," the man muttered. "Looking for a handout."

"Look at her. She's beautiful, Wilbur. We should give her something to eat."

"Forget it, Iris. We're not taking in another cat. I'm calling Animal Control in the morning." The man closed the blinds.

TOUGH GUYS

Caffeina went back to the others to report her failure.

"Where's Cicero?" she asked. "And Marco? Where's he?" No one seemed to be in charge.

"I'm going back out," she said. "I don't know where, but I'll keep looking until I find someone. Anybody else want to come?"

Tweezer moved to join her.

"Oh! What a pity." A voice from the ground stopped them in their tracks. "Looks like your precious library is burning." Sting was planted squarely under the tree, along with Tank, Crimmany and some out-of-towners.

"Hey scabs! I'm talking to you!"

"Scram, creep," yelled Tweezer.

"Oh, you must be the tough guy, huh?" accused Sting.

"What kind of tough guy hides in a tree?" asked Tank.

"In case you didn't notice, the books are burning," said Sting. "You gonna sit and watch? What a bunch of losers."

Tweezer climbed farther down the tree. "I'm not going to take this," he muttered under his breath.

"Don't go!" Caffeina whispered. "They'll kill you!"

There was a cracking sound inside as the table, where the fire had started, split and crashed to the floor.

"I love a good fire. Don't you?" Sting said to Tank. The other raccoons were milling restlessly about, looking in the windows.

"Hey, Sting!" yelled one of the newcomers. "I thought you said we were gonna have a good fight tonight. There's nobody here to fight with."

"Yeah, you're right. They're a bunch of nobodies."

"Scaredy cats. That's what they are."

"I know what'll get 'em down," taunted Sting. "Here, kitty, kitty. I have something special for you."

Sting went over to the bushes and yanked on the leash that Polo was tied to. "I got your ratty little pet here. Come and get 'em!"

Sting yanked Polo by his collar and held him up, squirming and strangling. Polo tried to squeal but nothing came out.

Tweezer took a flying leap off the branch. In one fell swoop, he grabbed the leash with his teeth and jerked it out of Sting's paw. The startled raccoon had no time to act and Polo, with the leash dragging behind him like a long tail, ran as far and as fast as he could.

A PURPOSE IN LIFE

Marco followed the gray cat to the rooftop. He wasn't sure what to do about the fire, but he was sure he needed to keep track of the raccoon turned cat. He moved stealthily behind him, but he needn't worry. Bait was too self absorbed.

Bait, the traitor, began a conversation with someone Marco couldn't see. Someone he was obviously friends with.

"I've failed. Cicero has vanished and so, I assume, has the Book. My plan to smoke him out seems childish now," Bait was saying. Marco tuned his hearing and another voice became audible.

"While you've been playing with fire, I've been speaking with my benefactor. He sends you a message."

"Yes?"

"He says we can give you something better than what you were looking for."

"What could that possibly be?" demanded Bait.

"A purpose. You simply need direction."

"What do I want with direction? I want my magic!" he said angrily.

"You don't need silly magic tricks like shape changing anymore! That's for beginners."

A chill wind wrestled with the leaves on the magnolia tree.

"Stop playing around like this is some kind of game!" said the whispery voice. "You are behaving like a timid house cat!"

"That is unfair!" cried Bait.

"Then don't bother me anymore. You don't want my advice."

"No. No! Don't go. Tell me," said Bait.

There was a long moment of silence before Marco heard them speak again.

"Think about it. You'll never get to the Book as long as it has a Guardian. He's only doing his job, you know, but he's getting too old. Maybe he was good once upon a time, but no longer. The Book needs someone younger and stronger. You... you are the worthy one!"

"Yes, it is by all rights, mine."

"That only proves his foolishness. His judgment is failing. It's time you stepped in and took action. You must not hesitate or falter now."

Marco smelled scorched paper and heard the crackle of burning books below mingled with the quiet sounds of treachery here on the roof.

"Cicero has been selfish, wanting to keep it all for himself. This is a Book to be shared and that will never happen as long as he is alive. You must have the courage to do what is necessary!"

A gust of wind whipped down from the roof and lightning from the approaching storm flared in the distance.

DESTINY HAS ITS OWN WAYS

An insignificant stone became the cause for change in the course of events. Gravity and vibration caused a small rock to dislodge and roll towards Marco. It was enough to catch Bait's attention. He whirled around, his yellow eyes glowing with a savagery he had kept hidden for so long under his gray cloak. "What are you doing here?"

"What are *you* doing? And who were you talking to?" asked Marco.

"None of your business," answered Bait.

"It is my business, if you are planning to kill Cicero."

"Oh! Aren't you the noble knight? Always out to save somebody. You're so pathetic. You don't have what it takes to be a Guardian, whatever foolish ideas Cicero put in your head. You'll never be anything more than a lap cat."

"I thought you were my friend, Bait. What happened to you?"

"I was never your friend, fool. You don't get it, do you? Grow up!"

Something below them crashed as the fire continued to gain strength. Lightening flashed and made them both jump.

"How could you burn the library?" demanded Marco. In the distance, the sound of thunder accompanied the faint whine of sirens. "What could possibly make you turn so..." bitter, he thought, then stopped as the realization hit him. "You were training, weren't you?"

"I'm still in training. I'm the rightful heir. You'll never take over."

"I'm not taking over anything."

"You are so naïve. You want to know what happened? You think Cicero is such a great and honorable cat? He's old and greedy and he'll turn on you like he did me. And he doesn't keep his word. How noble is that?"

"What happened to you, Bait? You were not like this when I first met you."

"No? Maybe not. Maybe I still had some hope in me. Like you. I thought I could get back into Cicero's good graces. But he shut me out... completely. Then you came along... not so corrupt as his old student... and I knew it was all over for me. He gave up on me. So I gave up trying."

Marco felt a sudden pang of sympathy for Bait. "I'm... "

"Don't," said Bait.

"Wha...?"

"Don't feel sorry for me. I can't stand it."

"You are heartless, even to yourself. I think that's the saddest part of this."

"I don't need your pity!" Bait suddenly leaped onto him and sank his teeth into Marco's leg. "There! You want to retract that touching bit of sympathy? Save it for Cicero—after I finish with him."

Bait backed up and crouched, ready for another attack. Marco ignored the pain and got himself into a better position. He didn't want to be caught off guard again and didn't wait to be attacked. He leaped on top of Bait and held his head between his paws, his sharp claws digging into the sides of Bait's face. Blood spurted out, making it harder for Marco to keep his hold. He slipped and rolled down the steep roof. The only thing that kept him from falling was the gutter.

He righted himself just as Bait pounced on top of him. Marco fell over the edge of the roof, barely grabbing hold of the gutter with his claws. Pain pierced through his body and he felt himself slipping toward certain death.

Bait came over to gloat at Marco's predicament. "Too bad for you. It's certain now that you'll never become a Guardian," he said. "But think of it this way. At least you've secured your legacy as one of the Dead Cats."

Bait put his full weight behind the punch he prepared to deal to Marco. It should have been the end of him, but a deafening crack of thunder and a high-voltage jolt of lightning split the sky open. Bait lost his concentration and his balance.

Rain poured from the sky and Marco heard the thud of Bait's body hit the ground sixty feet below.

DEAD CATS

"What's this?" cried Tank. "A dead cat?"

"One dead cat!" announced Crimmany, circling the body, like he was taking credit for his demise.

Tweezer and Caffeina came over to view the lifeless body. They stood there in the rain, sniffed and nudged him with their noses and looked at each other. What a strange thing that Bait had come to fall out of the sky with the rain, thought Tweezer.

"Aw. Poor kitty. Looks like you lost one of your pals," said Sting. "But save your crying for later. After you're all dead."

"That's a good one, Sting!" said Crimmany.

Sting was ignoring Crimmany and staring hard at Tweezer instead. Tweezer raised to his full height and more than met his look. "I believe we were in the middle of a fight," he said.

"Looks like you've lost more fights than you've won," Sting replied. "Just like you're going to lose this one."

"You've haven't seen my opponents when I'm done with them."

"Fightin' kitties doesn't count."

"I've wrestled with you before."

"Just warm up exercises."

The sound of sirens were in the background, growing louder. Tweezer tuned it out, so he could keep all his senses for the battle. He dared not look away from Sting, but he was aware of Tank and Crimmany. They flanked their leader on both sides. Then there was the two other raccoons hovering around the edges.

Tweezer moved to one side to keep his opponent slightly off balance.

"What's the matter? Cat got your tongue?" goaded Tank.

Caffeina, however, could not keep hers. "What's the matter with you Sting? Why do you enjoy making our lives miserable? We are peace-loving cats, but I'll tell you right now, you will be sorry you got on our bad side!"

"You cats are such comedians. I'm dying from laughter," said Crimmany.

The two combatants continued to size each other up, both on their haunches, thrusting paws in threatening gestures, each provoking the other into making the first move.

Tweezer had his eyes locked onto Sting, but he knew what was going on around him, as though he had eyes in the back of his head.

Caffeina saw the movement at the same time Tweezer did. "Tweezer! Watch out!" One of the raccoons at his back lurched forward to attack him.

Tweezer lunged forward to avoid the attack. At the same time, he shoved Crimmany into Sting's body with a force that took both raccoons down.

Tweezer whirled around to face the other raccoons, while Pudge, Skitzo and Caffeina had already tackled the other three.

But Tweezer soon realized they weren't home free. Raccoons came creeping out of the bushes, their eyes on fire. They swallowed up the very air around them and dove into the melee.

It was a noisy, riotous brawl and the cats were completely engulfed by their attackers, the odds totally against them.

No one saw Bait get up from his fall and slink away.

WOULD YOU LIKE SOMETHING FOR THE PAIN?

The thunder no longer came in soft rolls. It hit with deafening cracks and competed with the blare of sirens.

Marco was still on the roof, licking his wounds. He didn't care that he was getting soaked. His leg, badly bitten, was too painful for him to move. However, as torn and bloody as he was, he was satisfied he'd taken care of Bait. Actually, he was pretty proud of the way he'd handled the whole thing and couldn't wait to tell Cicero.

"You were lucky."

Marco jerked his head up in surprise. He saw only the rain hitting the dark tiles of the roof. The voice spoke again in a low murmur. "Lucky this time. Maybe not so lucky the next."

"Who are you?"

"I'm your inspiration."

"You are? Why can't I see you?"

"I work behind the scenes." Lighting streaked white veins across the black sky and Marco saw the blur of a shadow where the voice came from.

"Would you like something for the pain?" Without waiting for an answer, the shadow swept over and covered

Marco like a cloak. The pain disappeared and he no longer felt the rain falling on him.

"Isn't that better?"

"Yes, very nice," said Marco, feeling pleasantly drowsy.

"What are your plans now?"

"Plans? I don't know. I should find Cicero and see what can be done about putting out the fire."

"Don't worry. The firemen will take care of it."

"Good. That's very good," Marco answered groggily.

"We need to have a talk, Marco."

"We do? I just want to sleep."

"Yes, you will sleep soon enough. A nice, long nap. But first, I want to ask. Have you really thought about what it means to be a Guardian?"

"Sure." Marco peered out through half-opened eyes, wondering who he was talking to.

"You should be aware of some things. Can I tell you now?"

"Okay." Marco sighed contentedly. He felt happy and warm, in spite of being wet. It was nice to have someone to talk to.

"You should think about what it means to be a Guardian. For the rest of your life, you will be bound to the Book. You cannot leave it, put it aside, or go on a journey, even a short one. No matter what, you will spend the rest of your days as the library cat. Day after day. Year after year. It's not an exciting life. Not the life of adventure you had planned."

"Really? I hadn't thou…"

"I know you hadn't. That's why I'm here. To help you think."

"Oh, well thank you." Marco could barely stay awake and was not at all sure what this thing… or whoever was talking to him… was saying.

"You will never be able to tell anyone what you do. Not even the librarians will know. You will live in obscurity, petted by old women, tortured by small children. No one will appreciate your sacrifices."

"That doesn't sound…" Marco struggled to stay awake and think coherently.

"Exactly. I thought you should know. Being a Guardian is not anything like being a hero. It's more like being a slave."

Marco couldn't stay awake any longer. He closed his eyes and fell into a deep sleep.

When Marco woke later, the rain had stopped and Lily was licking his wounds.

"This looks bad," she said.

"It's nothing."

"It's a very deep wound. It could get infected."

"Really, I'm okay."

"Mum gave me some special things to say for wounds. It should heal up in no time."

Lily was so confident in her abilities that Marco surrendered. He was out of sorts but didn't know why. Slowly, the strange conversation he had on the roof came back to him.

"I heard that evil thing talking to you," she said.

"You did? You were here?"

"Yes, and I just want to tell you that you shouldn't listen to voices like that. They don't care about you. They don't care about anybody. They are mean and selfish and you'll end up just like Bait if you listen to them."

MEETINGS

Cicero went out the window. The cats and raccoons were having a knockdown drag-out fight on the lawn of the library, and fire was glowing through the windows. But Cicero was forced to leave it all behind and head for the Springs, where he hoped to find Alaniah to let him in the vault.

He crossed the rain-soaked street and was heading for the park when he encountered a lone cat.

"What's going on?"

"What do you mean?"

"Well, it's pretty noisy around here. Trouble?"

"I don't have time to talk." Cicero strained his neck to look ahead. He really needed to get moving again.

"Maybe I could help out."

"Go get in the middle of the brawl, if you like."

"Hey, you don't have to be rude."

Something about this cat was familiar in a disturbing way. "Do I know you?" Cicero cocked his head and really looked at the cat this time.

"No. I'm just passing through." He shrank back into the shadows a little.

Cicero didn't have time to worry about who this cat was. "Well, you should keep on going. There's nothing but trouble here right now."

"Not very friendly, are you?"

"No."

"I've heard rumors about the cats in this place."

"Yeah, what kind of rumors?" Cicero shifted impatiently.

"Something about dead cats... ghost cats. Weird and eccentric. You one of those?"

Cicero narrowed his eyes. "Who are you?"

"Just offering a friendly hand. You don't have to be so suspicious."

This made Cicero all the more suspicious. "Must be my eyes are playing tricks on me. You have the voice of another, but your fur is curious... it is wearing thin."

"You speak strangely. You *must* be one of the dead cats... or possibly one of the noble Guardians I have heard about."

"You have heard about the Guardians? Might you be a reader cat?"

"Most assuredly."

"Then you are more deceptive than I even imagined. How did you change your appearance in this way?"

"Your eyes are tricking you."

"I am not using only my eyes. There are other ways of seeing," said Cicero.

"You speak in such cryptic language. What do you have to hide?"

"Why do you ask? You know the answer already," said Cicero.

"Then…." the cat paused. "You should know what you did to me."

"What *I* did!" Cicero exclaimed. No pretense was possible now.

"Yes. What you did was unforgivable. What were you thinking when you abandoned me?"

"That's what you call it?" Cicero asked, his fury rising. "The dishonor of your actions was enough to disqualify you from the Dead Cats Society, let alone from becoming a Guardian."

"Then why didn't you kick me out? Why did you let me stay around, thinking there was some hope of regaining your trust?"

"Maybe I did have some hope."

"What was my big crime?"

"You wanted it too much," said Cicero. "This isn't a job anyone should desire. The responsibility is too great."

They made wide circles around each other, keeping their eyes locked together.

"This charade is enough to assure me that I made the right decision, if I ever doubted. What are you doing appearing in disguise? What are you hiding, dear Baitengirth?"

It seemed that his use of Bait's full name was his flashpoint. His old companion charged at him like some dreadful demon.

Cicero was not without resources for dealing with such things. A multitude of electrical charges remained in the air from the storm. When the fallen apprentice was only a breath way, Cicero drew power from the invisible currents and aimed them at Bait.

The changeling cat disappeared without a trace.

BEAT 'EM WITH FRIES

Polo ran randomly through yards and across parking lots, dodging cars and dogs and a baby carriage. He was not tired of running, especially since he'd been tied up so long, but a thought stopped him. It wasn't something that happened very often, but he thought about how Tweezer had saved his life and how he and the others were fighting the raccoons. The cats were in trouble and here he was, running away. What was he doing here under a tree, when they needed his help?

He didn't think any further, like what chance a silly ferret would have in fending off a dozen gangster raccoons. He chewed on what was left of the leash, thinking more than he'd ever thought in his life, when he heard footsteps. When they got close enough, Polo saw it was a pack of mangy cats.

"Hey!" one called out.

Polo loped over to meet them.

"Maybe you could give us directions?"

"Depends on where you want to go," said Polo.

"The library."

"I just came from the library, and I don't think you want to go there now."

"Why not?" asked one of the cats.

"The library's on fire and there's a pack of raccoons in a brawl with the cats."

"That's the place."

"Really?"

"We're friends of Tweezers. He asked for backup and we're it."

"Tweezer could use some help, but I have to tell you, those raccoons are brutal, and I don't know that you could do much good."

"Well, we're here now. We have to do something."

Polo decided to tell them what he'd been pondering. "I've been thinking of trying a diversionary tactic," he said. It was a term he'd learned from Marco, and he'd been waiting for a chance to use it.

"Say what?"

"You know, a way to take their attention away from the cats, with something they want more than fighting."

"Well, you seem to know so much. What do you think would get their attention?"

"Simple," said Polo. "Raccoons are pigs. They love to eat more than anything. We'll tempt them with food."

"Brilliant idea. But how do you propose we get food to them? We're cats. It's not like we can steal food and lug it over there."

Polo smiled. "That's why you need me."

The one cat who seemed to be the group's leader brought the rest of them into a huddle. Then he went back to Polo. "Okay. Here's the deal. We weren't gonna come, 'cause we like our lives and don't want anything to mess with that. Understand? But some of us got to thinking about what Tweezer and Caffeina said, and it made sense. We'd want help if we were in trouble. So here we are, but we don't have much of a plan. So, we took a vote. We'll go with your plan."

Polo suddenly found himself in charge of a troupe of cats. He puffed up with pride. "First thing we need to do is scope out some food. Anything will do. They are not picky eaters." He almost added, 'not like cats,' but caught himself in time.

Boris sniffed the air. "I smell french fries."

"Take us to the fries, then," commanded Polo, and they followed Boris to a dumpster.

Polo scaled the large bin in a flash. The cats waited below.

"Here, catch!" He tossed bags of fries over the side until he was satisfied they all had one. He secured one in his mouth and hopped down.

"Follow me." The cats each had a bag clenched in their teeth and they trotted down the street, surely a strange sight if anyone had been looking out their window.

Once they made it to the library, only Polo was brave enough to get close to the raccoons and let them get a whiff. But it was enough. The first raccoon picked up the scent and lost interest in fighting. The stray cats dropped their bags and beat a hasty retreat.

The raccoons knocked each other over to get the fries, leaving the Dead Cats stunned but grateful.

THINGS LEFT UNSAID

The fire had been quelled before any major damage occurred. The entire newspaper section was reduced to ashes, but it was the smoke which created the greatest hazard, and the library had to be closed for several days. Cicero slept uneasily in the magnolia tree, which did not suit him in the least. Marco kept him company.

"Were you scared?" asked Marco. "Didn't it remind you of the fire at Alexandria? I couldn't believe my eyes when I saw Bait setting the fire. How could he change so much? I swear, he looked like a raccoon at first. And up on the roof, he was talking to a shadow who wanted him to kill you. The whole thing was so weird. But I stopped him! I would never let anyone hurt you, Cicero."

"Thank you, dear Marco," Cicero said wearily. "You have proven yourself worthy. I have chosen well after all."

Marco had stopped short of telling Cicero about his own conversation with the Whisperer. He couldn't tell him how close he'd come to walking away from the whole thing. It was impossible to think of it now without cringing. If it weren't for Lily, well... he didn't want to think about it.

Cicero wasn't telling everything, either. He never told Marco about his own encounter with Bait, preferring to let Marco enjoy his victory. He would need this triumph to build on for the future.

But why hadn't he used the power of the book to *do* something? He'd gone after Alaniah, but he could have done something else. Why was he so incompetent? Was it age? Was he losing his power so gradually he didn't even notice? No, he'd had the presence of mind to use it to defeat Bait. Still, he was alarmed at how weak and tired he felt.

MISS PINKLEY

In spite of the library being officially closed, it was busier than usual. Insurance adjustors, fire inspectors, police and health officials nosed around with clipboards.

When Professor Chin arrived for the purpose of examining the older manuscripts, Miss Pinkley assumed he was sent by someone higher up.

She was rather taken with him, even though she would never have admitted it. Maybe it was the fedora, or his square jaw and solemn face punctuated by a trim moustache. It could have been his soft-spoken manner. But most likely it was the eye patch which suggested an intriguing past. He carried a large leather satchel, not in a casual way, like a lot of people, but as though it held his most precious possessions.

He inquired about the location of older books and manuscripts, offering his condolences to her about the fire. He said he hoped they didn't lose anything too valuable, but this was his area of expertise and he would be able to give her a full report.

"Oh," said Miss Pinkley. "There's also a small collection upstairs. I don't know if you're interested in that one. It's mostly local history, but there are some very old books in that room. We were worried about the smoke damage since it collected in the balcony area, but our big concern was Cicero."

"Cicero?"

"Oh," laughed Miss Pinkley, wondering at the sudden paleness that came over the man. "Cicero is our library cat. He pretty much owns the local history room."

"Maybe I could start there. Yes, that would be good."

"Certainly Professor. I'll show you where it is." Miss Pinkley got up, happy with the opportunity to escort the man to the room, but stopped short when an insurance adjustor approached her with some questions.

"Don't worry," Professor Chin assured her. "I'll find my way."

Miss Pinkley sighed. "We are getting ready to go home for the night. You only have a short time left today."

LEGACIES

Professor Chin entered the small room crammed with old books, many lying in piles on a long polished wood table. It was untidy, obviously not kept up to standards, he thought, but then this wasn't the British Library, was it? The sight of the cat, even sleeping on a green velvet chair, caught his breath. The click of the metal latch as he closed the door behind him startled the cat into wakefulness.

"I thought you might be dead by now, after that trick you pulled in London," said the Professor.

The cat bolted upright, back arched. Professor Chin smiled benevolently at Cicero. "But of course, you must have nine lives like any normal cat."

He brushed the dampness collecting on his palms onto his coat. "You probably never thought I'd find you in this backwater place. But I don't give up, once I have a purpose and besides..." He lowered his shoulder, letting his satchel slide to the table, and thought about how much he should reveal. But, he laughed, what was he worried about? After all, he was only talking to a cat. He kept his tone friendly. "I have extra help now, the Finders. Creatures who travel without passports or reservations; they have no boundaries in time or space. You'll never be able to hide your Book well enough to evade them."

He paced along the table's edge, never losing sight of Cicero, careful not to make him too nervous. Careful even more so, not to give in to his rage. The cat was again standing in his way. He loathed having to negotiate with this vicious creature once again.

The Finders had led him here but wouldn't... or couldn't... tell him the exact location of the Book. He considered their services inadequate for the price he paid and would take his revenge on them when he had the power to do so. But he'd think about that later. The cat was growling at him.

He stepped to the far side of the table, calculating, despising. "It's been a long time. Do you even remember me? Maybe you need a reminder." He removed his fedora and placed it on top of the satchel.

"Every morning, when I look in the mirror, I remember you."

Professor Chin reached behind his head and pulled his eye patch off.

"Every morning, I am forced to wear this to cover my scarred and useless eye."

The cool air hit the moist, shrunken pulp of his empty eye socket. "It's your legacy to me, but I have a legacy for you as well." He replaced his eye patch and returned the fedora to cover his head. "My legacy to you, dear Cicero, is a curse. I will create a special one and place it upon you until the end of time."

LANGUAGE OF THE UNSEEN

Cicero was pretty sure he could escape being captured by Professor Chin, but the dark form slinking around the room, little more than a shadow, he wasn't so sure about. He still had nightmares about these creatures that seemed to follow the Professor like evil pets. Now even the books seemed to recoil in horror from the presence of this madman.

But, on closer examination, he saw this wasn't one of the creatures that almost smothered him when Professor Chin had trapped him in a cage in London. This time, there was only one, and it had a voice.

At the same time, the Professor was coaxing him with artificially sweetened words. "Come on, old man. You've had your distinguished career as the library cat. None of the librarians will know what happened. What do they know anyway? I will relieve you of your duties and you will be free to read your dusty old tomes."

Cicero jumped off the chair and began to walk in a wide circle around the Professor, hissing.

"You foolish cat! You think you can intimidate me! How absurd! Oblige me and I will grant you peace. Cross me and not only will I destroy you, I will destroy the preposterous notion of the legendary Guardian Cats."

Cicero continued to circle the Professor, who turned in order to keep his one good eye on him.

"Shall I bring in my companions?" threatened the man. "I must warn you. I can't always control them."

Cicero stopped moving and began to speak directly to the Professor, translating his words into the language of the Unseen, one he knew the Professor would understand. "I will never reveal the Book to you! I will not make that mistake again."

The Professor sighed. "That is truly unfortunate… just as we are getting reacquainted." To the Voice, as Cicero thought of it, the Professor said, "He's resisting me. Now we must get serious."

Cicero had no idea what he would be up against this time, but whatever the Professor had in mind was certain to be grim.

THE COLOR OF HUMANS

Marco was outside Cicero's chamber. This was the first time he'd ever seen it closed and he pawed and meowed at the door. He heard a man's voice on the other side and smelled an unfamiliar, bitter smell.

After a bit, the librarian appeared. "Oh dear, this will never do, will it Marco? Cicero hates being locked in." She opened the door and poked her head in briefly, "Professor, we'll be closing in fifteen minutes. And, if you don't mind, we like to keep the door open for our library cats."

Miss Pinkley left and Marco scurried into the room. From behind the velvet chair he had a good view of the man. He blinked once, then again, but it didn't change what he saw. Most humans came in shades of blue or green. This one was surrounded by a smoky haze and seemed to be talking to an even darker shapeless being.

Cicero walked over to sit beside him. In a tone heavy with regret, Cicero spoke. "Of all the stories, I have not told you the one I really should have. But it didn't seem possible that this mad man would find me again. So far from home."

Marco knew this was not the time to ask questions and was grateful that Cicero seemed anxious to explain.

"I am old and I fear I must pass my duties on to you while you are still a novice." As usual, Cicero's explanations raised more questions than answers. What do you mean? he wanted to ask. Who is this man and why is he such a strange color?

Cicero was talking, but Marco was being drawn in by the man's chanting of words in a strange language.

Cicero scolded him. "Marco! Do not listen to his dark words. They will affect you in a bad way. It can take a great deal of force—to resist the darkness. Menacing words have their own power, whispering promises and pretending to be your friend. Remember when I was telling you about the power of an idea?"

With effort, Marco turned his head away from the man's hypnotic presence towards Cicero. "Humans are their caretakers, but some ideas are born in a bad place, an unbalanced mind. Once implanted, they can fester and feed off old wounds. This dark creature before us—the Professor—has fed and nurtured a bad idea, untamed by the counsel of wiser men, and so it has become a monster."

The Professor walked in a circle around the room, turning within his own shadow as he went, and followed by another one. He continued his incantations in an unctuous manner, like a man obsessed with his own importance.

"He is no longer even its caretaker but he has become its slave. *The Book of Motion* in the hands of such a madman! We must do everything necessary to prevent these two forces from coming together. *The Book of Motion* does not recognize the intentions of its possessor."

The Professor extended one arm, tilting his head slightly, aligning his good eye to his pointed finger, as though looking through the site of a rifle. He turned in a 360-degree circle, his finger leaving a raven-colored trail, so that when he completed the turn, he was encircled by a dark ring.

When Cicero shivered, Marco shivered automatically. He tried to crouch closer to the floor in a futile attempt to avoid the wave of cold, dead air that filled the room.

But there was no avoiding the creature the Professor summoned with the final words of his incantation. "From your world into this world... Enter! Come now and make your presence known!"

IN THE ABODE WHERE DEMONS LINGER

In a place where the Seen and Unseen worlds merge, in the abode where demons linger, preparing for invasions, a black dog-like creature with glowing yellow eyes surfaced into the library.

His foul odor curled Cicero's nose.

"Welcome, Bodis," Professor Chin said.

"Where am I?" snarled the dog.

"In the library of a hidden treasure."

"What do I care for pirates' booty?" the dog snapped.

"This treasure is worth more than gold—a Book that will give me power over men's minds."

"A useful book for a change. But what do you need me for?"

"You see this cat," he said, pointing to Cicero. "He guards the treasure and refuses to give me the key."

The dog whipped his fire-tail around, radiating sparks. "You want me to make him talk?"

"I think you could persuade him."

Cicero's first instinct was to back up, but there was nowhere to go and he had nothing to lose. He spoke to the Professor, "Your command of the dark creatures is impressive. But why bring them back now? They've been behind the wall for eons. You must know how dangerous they are in this world. Even to their commander."

"They make useful companions," said the Professor.

Cicero hissed, "Your intentions are the vilest of any human. There is nothing in this world that would compel me to let you even get close to the Book!"

The Professor turned slightly in the direction of the hell hound and swept his arm in a wide arc toward Cicero. The dog obeyed and charged. Cicero leaped straight up, scrambling to keep his hold on the bookshelves. But the hound was in close pursuit, climbing the shelves in a clumsy but relentless chase, singeing Cicero with fire blasts from his tail and spewing saliva over books tumbling to the floor in his wake.

HIDEOUS BEAST

Marco vaulted up and over the velvet chair onto the hound's back and dug his claws into the animal's hideous body.

The beast continued to scale the bookshelves lathered by the hunt and his bloodthirsty nature. When all three creatures were at the top, Cicero escaped in a flying leap to the floor, barely avoiding the dog's dagger-like fangs.

Marco was still gripped on the back of the demon animal as the dog inelegantly climbed down from the shelves. Cicero was struggling to get up from his fall, but by the time Marco was on the ground, Cicero had hobbled up to the low shelf under the window and climbed to the sill. He seemed to be waiting for the dog to notice him, and then he jumped out the window. What in the world was he doing?

When the dog leaped through the opening after Cicero, Marco had no intention of letting go, and so he sailed through the air on the dog's back. All three of them crashed in a heap on the ground, with Cicero on the bottom. When the beast of a dog arose, the old Guardian lay motionless on the ground, his head and neck twisted, his fur smoldering.

At first Marco couldn't understand what had happened to Cicero, and then a ferocious cry pierced the air. It took a minute to realize the sound he heard came from him.

The hound twisted his head back, seeming to realize for the first time something was fastened onto him. Marco knew he was doomed, but if he let go, he felt the dog would eat him alive.

The hound flung himself into a frenzy trying to dislodge him, but Marco was latched on, his head laid flat against the thick roll of fur and skin on the dog's neck. His eyes were closed tight and he tried not to breathe in the dog's stench.

Somehow in the middle of this madness, he thought he saw Cicero, looking alive. He was speaking to him, but Marco couldn't understand what he was saying. The dog was throwing himself against the magnolia tree, smashing Marco's back against the trunk.

"The words, Marco!" said Cicero's apparition.

The dog started to spin in circles.

Marco tried to hear what his mentor was saying.

"Remember the words!"

The words! He couldn't imagine the words could help him now. He only remembered what a disaster it had been the last and only time he tried saying them. But he had no other options. "*Faw...*" he began, and with the utterance of that sound, he noticed a change, but it wasn't for the better.

The hound was rolling in the dirt, frantically trying to dislodge him.

227

"*Fawta...lani,*" he continued haltingly.

The dog's fangs clamped on to his hind leg and Marco clawed his way farther up so he was practically on top of the dog's head.

"*Nee!*" The last word exploded from within him and he suddenly found himself airborne, still clinging to the hell hound. The ascent was swift and the pair twisted and swung violently in midair.

Marco lost his grip and fell. He landed on all fours and looked up to see what had happened to the dog. He had been snatched up by an enormous bird, something like an eagle, but with a body like a lion. The hell hound hung loosely in the talons of this strange flying creature. Marco sat motionless until both bird and dog disappeared in the sky, leaving him wondering if what just happened was a dream. When he returned to Cicero's lifeless body, however, he knew it was no dream.

THE PERFECT SOCIETY

The Professor turned away from the window. Half-witted hellhound, he thought. He was only supposed to extort information from Cicero, not kill him. He needed more control over his creatures. Now what would he do?

He hid out in the bathroom while the library shut down for the night. The mousy librarian would just assume he'd slipped out while she was busy. Besides, he thought with a smile, librarians would never suspect his kind of deception, except in books.

His palms were sweating again and he reached in his pocket for his handkerchief. It wasn't there, which made him panic. Things were not going as planned and this small detail, the fact that he'd forgotten it, only increased his anxiety. He couldn't afford any more mistakes.

He washed his face and hands and dried them thoroughly on the scratchy brown paper towel, refocusing on his quest. Hitler had his Spear of Destiny. He had obviously unlocked its secrets and would have ruled the world if... Well, he wouldn't make the same mistakes Hitler made.

In his world, no one would ever die. People would pay dearly to join. It would be the perfect society because no one ever wanted to die. With an elite team of doctors and scientists working under his direction, he would exceed where all tin pot dictators had failed.

Calmed somewhat, he opened the bathroom door slightly. The library was darkened except for the green glow of the exit lights.

The Book was here, his 'Book of Destiny'. There was no doubt that it belonged to him. He had been chosen. Once it was his, he would unlock its secrets and his dreams would come true. He would become the greatest magician of all time. Not a charlatan stage magician, but the kind who work behind the scenes, the ones who have the real power in the world.

Yes, he would be able to change himself to appear like anyone or anything he wanted, if the legends about the book were true. He erased that moment of doubt quickly from his mind. He'd come this far. The Finders and his Whisperer had helped him. It had to be true. It was his destiny, he felt it stronger than anything he'd ever felt and allowed himself to contemplate his future. Being able to appear however he liked would mean he could gain access to anyone, have the ear of any of the world's leaders. With a jolt, he suddenly realized even Hitler himself could have been under his power!

He would have underlings do his dirty work and take the brunt of people's anger. They wouldn't mind, because he would hold their life in his hands. They would never have to face the awful prospect of death. They would be only too willing to do his bidding for the small exchange of their soul.

He walked slowly through the stacks, scraping his finger along the book spines. He couldn't really imagine how a cat thought, but he had the notion that the book might be hidden in plain sight. It was worth exploring.

On a short, round table surrounded by orange plastic chairs was a children's book with cartoon demons on the cover. Children made his skin crawl. They were disgusting and unmanageable and had no idea what a real demon looked like.

Other children's books repelled him. Why would anyone want to go *Fishin' with Grandpa?* He never let himself wonder if his childhood was tarnished. He rarely thought about it except when he caught a glimpse of the scars on his back. His throat tightened and he felt like he needed air.

Maybe the Book would be hidden in the history section. He located the Dewey Decimal numbers beginning with 930, histories of the ancient world, and began randomly pulling books off the shelves, throwing them on the floor. A rising sense of panic made him shudder and he had to calm himself again. He could not allow himself to lose control or let fear grab hold of him. He went down each aisle, randomly stabbing at books and creating holes in the order of things.

How could he be so close and not find it? He cursed Cicero for dying before he got the secret to its location. He cursed the demon beast for not obeying him. Then he cursed the library for hiding the Book.

Then logic prevailed. If the library would not cooperate, he would punish it. He got his book of spells from his satchel and found the curse. *"Murraq-di-fih cum-dan...i-fi..."*

He moved through the library, making friends with the dark words, feeling their power grow with each repetition. Faint sounds came from within the library books, like the crackling of brittle paper. He kept moving through the stacks, unphased by cries and shouts. He began to enjoy the noise when he realized what it was, and just to commemorate the moment, he bowed to the characters as they began emerging from the books, trying to escape certain death.

"Murraq-di-fih, cum-dan-fi, re-quin-i-fi..." Louder this time. He repeated the chant over and over, amazed at his strength. The library was crumbling and he had performed this marvelous feat! The transformation took place before his eyes. When he had finished, the main hall looked like a tomb for dead books—a crypt, filled with corpses of characters who would never tell their story again.

He congratulated himself.

At first he didn't recognize the figure in the mirror but it was dark. He checked the eyes staring back at him. Yes, they were his eyes, now yellow and glowing. This pleased him as well as the now-familiar metallic flavor on his tongue, a taste that accompanied his successes. A voice interrupted his self-admiration.

"You might need my help now," said his Whisperer.

"Why? I'm doing well on my own."

"You are looking *at* the mirror."

"What's your point?"

"What do you know about mirrors?"

Of course! How stupid of him. The door had been here the whole time. How could he have missed it?

"I have companions who will assist you," hissed the Whisperer.

Suddenly the temperature dropped. The mirror reflected a ghostly phantom behind him and before he could blink, he was wrapped in a shroud and pulled through the portal, with barely enough time to notice the other creatures who gleefully trailed along for the free ride.

THE WEIGHT OF A GUARDIAN

Marco arrived in Cicero's empty chamber, heavy with sadness and the weight of his new position. He never realized that becoming a Guardian meant losing his mentor and friend.

Feeling as though he'd been charged with protecting more than *The Book of Motion*, he walked out to the balcony, Cicero's old command post. He remembered how the old cat used to sit here for long hours, surveying the library as though he were the captain of his ship.

At first, he saw the dust in the air and confused it for smoke. He panicked, then quickly realized his mistake. But it might as well have been smoke—the library was in ruins.

He stood frozen to the floor, denying as long as possible that what his eyes saw was real. He wanted a closer look, because he couldn't distinguish anything recognizable. Mounds of rubble were everywhere and some sort of confetti floated in the air.

He descended the staircase, every step sinking him deeper in despair. Shafts of moonlight coming through the window blinds sliced through plumes of dust. When he reached the ground floor, he saw the crumbling debris of what used to be books spilling off the shelves, disintegrated into pulp. The ones left standing had cracked and peeling covers.

He had no doubt that the evil Professor's hand was in this, but he could not imagine what darkness lay within a human being who would annihilate a library . He thought of Alexandria and remembered hearing the cheers of men who celebrated the destruction of other men's stories.

He climbed over the mounds of rubble in a daze. It wasn't until a woman's face peered out from the debris that he realized he'd been climbing over dead bodies. The woman was wrapped in a brown fur coat, now covered in a layer of ashy white powder. He looked out across the floor where the dust was clearing and saw the mounds for what they really were. Corpses. There was something odd about how they laid all in the same direction, as if they had collapsed in the same moment, just before reaching the wide front door.

Marco wandered the battle field. There were World War II soldiers carrying rifles, as well as women in ball gowns. There were men in baseball caps and top hats, women in flowered hats and scarves, and little girls in braids. There were boys with slingshots, pirates and circus clowns, all victims of a battle of good and evil they had lost.

Marco didn't know how he knew, but it became obvious. The bodies were characters trying to escape the unspeakable horror of the death of their story.

He could go no further. He lay down between a circus clown and a cowboy and covered his head. He might as well be dead, too.

A shower of sparks rained down on him. Alaniah flew in circles around his head. "What are you doing in such a sorry state?"

Marco did not want to be confronted with his 'sorry state' and kept his head under the clown's polka dot suit.

"Marco, do you think Cicero left you in charge so you could bury your head when things got tough?"

"I didn't know it would get this bad," he said.

"You think this is a walk in the park, as humans say, protecting such a powerful Book?"

He pulled his head out from under the clown, ready to argue. "I don't know what I thought, but it wasn't this."

Alaniah laughed. "You're so funny, Marco. It will be interesting being your companion."

"How can you say that? I'm not fit to be a Guardian. I haven't completed my training. Alaniah, I have barely begun my training. I can't do this!"

"If not you, then who?"

Marco fell silent. She had a good point, but he didn't like it.

"You are not without resources," she insisted.

"What do you mean?"

"Ah, it never fails to amaze me how short are the memories of earthly creatures. Cicero gave you a gift, didn't he?"

"The words?"

"Of course, the words! Don't you remember what happened when you spoke them?"

Marco remembered when he spoke them last—the demon beast who killed Cicero had been plucked from this world by a gryphon.

"Don't forget these words."

"How are words going to change this, Alaniah? Look at the library. It's dead. Cicero's dead. I wish I were dead."

"Oh, youngling. You are so dramatic. Do you want this to be the end of your story?"

It was not a question. It was a challenge, and next to the ones Cicero had given him, these were probably the most powerful words Marco had ever heard. Their magic worked. No, he did not want this to be the end of his story!

"Words have power," Alaniah said. "From the beginning of time, they have brought things to life. All it takes to bring the library back is the belief in their power. Words brought darkness to this place and it will be words that bring it back."

Renewed, Marco ran back to the balcony for a better vantage point, Alaniah floating above him.

"Fa-taw-la-nee, rah-ma-la-nee, ma-fa-la-nee, moon-too-laaaah." He kept repeating the words, but nothing happened.

Then he saw something scurry out from between one set of stacks and down another. Could it be another raccoon? He ignored it, thinking that he had bigger problems than raccoons, but he was unprepared for what happened next.

The creature who had rescued him from the hell hound, a gryphon, flew in from a far corner and landed on the top of a high shelf, where he preened his talons and feathers and fur. Marco was mesmerized by the magnificent creature, so much so that even as it flew towards him, and even as it attacked him, he was completely stunned. The bird-beast's talons dug into Marco's skin, gripping him as he plucked him from the ground. All Marco could think was that this creature saved him only to return and make him his prey.

The gryphon landed on top of a high shelf and released Marco from his talons. But Marco was not free; he lay stretched out, the gryphon holding him down by standing on him with his full weight.

Marco imagined that the beast would begin to pick him apart, piece by piece. Some magic that was; the words had done him no good. Here he was doomed to die, a little bit at a time. He knew it was useless to struggle, that it would only speed the process.

When the bird-beast moved his head down towards him, Marco closed his eyes. Not that it would help, but it was the only thing he was able to move. The gryphon's beak parted his fur and Marco felt its razor sharp point on his skin.

It wasn't until the gryphon had been combing over his body for several moments that Marco realized he wasn't going to be eaten. He opened his eyes. The bird was grooming him.

When the gryphon finished, he remained on top of Marco, with his long tail waving gently down the side of the bookshelves. The bird bowed and touched his forehead to Marco's head, and oddly enough, something about this gesture reminded Marco of Cicero.

The gryphon picked him up and flew back down, deposited Marco on the floor, then flapped his enormous wings and flew off.

ANGEL IN DISGUISE

"Don't you just love the library?" said Lily.

Marco was shocked to find her sitting calmly, not two feet away. "How long have you been here?"

"Long enough to know I can't tell anybody what just happened."

Lily never ceased to amaze Marco. She seemed much older than the small white kitten she appeared to be.

Alaniah arrived in a shower of light. "Marco, there is no time to dawdle. You have work to do. I will open the door," she said. They had been standing by the mirror and Marco and Lily were suddenly pulled through the portal and onto the steps down to the dark, dungeon-like chamber.

A cold draft greeted them. "Where do you think you're going?" a voice whispered, and the cold air blew against Marco's face.

Marco turned to Lily. "I don't think you should be here." Lily ignored him and kept walking steadily down the stairs next to him. The further down they got, the dimmer the light became. Marco looked around for Alaniah, but it seemed they were on their own.

The stairway, which he had seen before, looked very different now. The rock walls glowed with lights, dozen of small ones in pairs, like eyes. Then Marco realized they *were* eyes, imprisoned in the rock.

Heat radiated from the wall on one side, and currents of cold air rose up from the depths of the dark canyon on the other side, making their passage miserably hot and cold at the same time. The eyes followed their every move down the steps. Marco was terrified, but he held to his course.

Just before the stairs took a sharp turn into total darkness, they reached the landing area. The door to the chamber was cracked open and the Professor was pacing around the table, chanting. The room was crowded with shadow creatures watching the Professor as he tried to take the Book. Electrical charges shattered the darkness of the room whenever he reached for it, and the Professor cursed the light.

Without warning, a shadow creature stretched one arm through the door and grabbed Lily. Marco lost sight of her within the shadow's murk until it plunked her down on the table next to the Book.

"What?" cried the Professor. "Where did this come from?" He grabbed Lily and held her by her neck. Lily struggled to breathe.

"Might you be an angel in disguise?" asked the Professor, laughing at his own joke. "A wicked cat is just what I need right now."

The Professor put her on the table in front of the Book and used her as a shield to absorb the shock. It didn't work. The power of the Book pushed them both back and a swirl of light escaped from the Book. Lily shook violently.

Marco didn't wait to see what the Professor would do next. In a flying leap he was on the table next to her.

"Is this my lucky day? Or am I cursed?" he asked.

"I daresay it is Cicero's young protégé," said the Whisperer.

"How did so many wretched cats get in here?"

The Professor swooped down and seized Marco, who pumped his hind legs furiously against the man's chest.

"Oh, no you don't! I'll not suffer from the claws of a cat again."

The Professor gripped both sets of Marco's legs while Marco tried to bite him.

"So wild. He must be feral," rasped the Whisperer.

"Feral cats in the library? I think they are not wild, but why are they lurking everywhere? The one I thought I needed is dead. Now...! How many more demon cats prowl this library?"

Marco turned his head so he could see Lily. Never had he seen her scared, not even in the clutches of Sting, but she was frightened now.

"Perhaps you could do something interesting with him? Try out some of your new skills," offered the Whisperer. "Better yet, use him for a spell needing a cat. Of course, he would have to be dead first."

Marco struggled to escape the Professor's grasp, trying every trick he knew. He finally got his head into a good position and sunk his teeth into the man's hand.

The Professor shrieked and threw him across the room. "Here, you take care of this beast," the Professor ordered the shadow. Before Marco could move, he was enveloped in a cold, black nothingness.

Like his dream. It *was* his dream, his nightmare come true!

He thrashed out in all directions, but it was impossible to fight an enemy he couldn't see. He heard the Professor's muffled voice as though he were under a heavy blanket. He heard nothing from Lily.

Then even within the darkness, Marco saw a flash of light and heard Lily's terrified yowl. The Professor announced, "You are mine!" and Marco knew he had the Book.

The shadow creature shifted positions and Marco couldn't tell if he was upside down or right side up. He was cold beyond belief and shivered so violently his teeth were chattering.

Then he realized the Professor was speaking to him, as though from the other side of a door. "You can have your freedom now," the man was saying. "It won't hurt a bit." Then he said something Marco couldn't hear as though he'd turned away. "All you must do is declare your allegiance to me." Suddenly the darkness cleared and Marco saw the Professor, but he was unable to move. "That's better. You can see me now. So let's get this over with quickly. I need to move on, but I want to test out my power. You will do as well as the next miserable creature."

The Book of Motion was lying open on the table and Lily was lying unconscious next to it. Or was she dead?

"Declare your obedience and, as much as I'd like to be rid of you, I will give you your mobility. You would like to walk again, wouldn't you?"

Marco struggled to move, but his body was as good as dead.

"You want to make this difficult? Don't waste my time. You are nothing to me and I will leave you down here to rot. Declare your obedience or suffer the consequences."

Marco could not imagine owing his life to this demon human, but he could also not allow the man to get away with possessing the Book and leaving Lily for dead. He was powerless and thought that maybe this was his sacrifice. Would he have to be the servant of a mad man in order to save the Book? Could the Professor unlock the secrets of the Book? Any power that his man had would be dangerous. That he had seen with his own eyes.

The Professor approached Marco and peered into his face. "My father always said the only good cat was a dead cat. I will make better use of you that way."

The Professor grabbed him by the throat and squeezed his neck. Somehow, through the terror, or maybe because of it, he remembered.

The words came to him and strength welled up inside. "Fa-taw-la-nee…" came the words that had mystical power, words that were the key to motion born from the beginning of time. It moved through his body and into his throat. The force that came out of his mouth bellowed like a lion.

Before he sprang, he recoiled and roared again, a terrible and savage cry.

In the small room there was only the lion, the man, the Book and a shivering white kitten. As a lion, Marco filled most of the empty space.

When he opened his mouth he spoke in the language of men. "Leave it! You have no permission to use this Book!"

The Professor was trying his best to appear unruffled, but when Marco roared the third time, the Professor backed up.

"This is not a book for magicians!" bellowed Marco, the lion-hearted.

"I will use it to help others," he offered, as if this would somehow appease the terrifying predator that stood before him. "People will be happy with my illusions."

"You seek to control the minds of men?" accused Marco.

"There is nothing greater than absolute power over other men," said the Professor.

"Your words echo those of tyrants and oppressors."

"Rulers, misunderstood, are often considered tyrants."

"You are nothing but a petty thief longing to become a god!" Marco growled. Then he opened his mouth to roar again, but instead a light appeared, filling the room. When it touched the Professor, the man appeared to shrink. He withdrew from the light and crouched in a corner, a small, pathetic creature. Like a battered child, thought Marco, and he had one fleeting glimpse into the man's wounded past.

Marco moved to the table and lowered his shoulders so Lily could easily climb on. Then he picked up the Book in his powerful jaws and went out to the landing area outside the door. Alaniah appeared on the steps.

"Where have you been?" roared Marco.

"I have my job, dear Marco, and you have yours. Forgive me if I am neglectful." Alaniah secured the door to the underground chamber, committing the Professor to utter darkness.

From the outside, Marco heard another door slam shut. Then a noise, like waves crashing, or the sound of steel gates rolling shut, and the screaming of a madman.

Rejoicing

Marco ascended the stone steps with Lily nestled in his lion's mane.

"I would never have believed that if I hadn't seen it with my own eyes," said Lily.

Alaniah lighted their way and Lily kept chattering all the way up. "You had light coming out of your mouth! How'd you do that, Marco?"

He moved with quiet strength and grace. As a lion, he could conquer anything. As the king of beasts, he could not imagine returning to being a stray cat of no consequence. Now he could protect the Book, the library, even the other cats.

Aware of every sinew in his powerful body, he shook his head, feeling the fan of fur that was his mane, almost unsettling Lily. He roared with the pride of this power, reveling in his new size and stature.

"You're scaring me Marco," said Lily. "But I like it."

When they reached the top step, Alaniah said, "You have done well, Marco, but your rejoicing will be short-lived."

Puzzling words, thought Marco, as he waited for her to open the portal. When she did, he stepped into the library, and indeed, his rejoicing moment was over.

As if such a thing were possible, the library seemed more desolate than before.

Encounter with the Queen

The stench of death was in the air and the only color present was varying shades of gray. Marco gently released the book from his jaws onto a table and Lily hopped off his back. He turned towards the sound of something like a pig rooting in the dirt, and a creature crawled out from between the ruined stacks.

Marco had only seen trolls in books before. The misshapen creature, looking like something cursed, ignored everything around him while he squatted on a children's table, picking things off his hairless body.

What seemed like an empty dead room now started filling up with small hairy beasts and dozens of gremlins. They appeared out of nowhere and roamed the library like rival gangs, sweeping books off the shelves, sending some whizzing across the room like missiles.

The wart-covered troll seemed oblivious to the riot, scooting across the floor until he reached the lion and began to sniff at him. Marco growled, warning him to keep his distance. The troll broke into a fit of damp sneezes and ran from the room, but not without leaving behind a putrid smell.

Not far from where the troll disappeared, a Queen emerged. She wore a dress of dazzling white underneath her red cape, and her crown sparkled so brightly it made Marco blink.

The Queen stepped over the dead bodies of the characters. The gremlins and warty things slunk off as she shooed them off with a black and gold scepter.

"Disgusting creatures, aren't they?" She aimed the scepter at Marco. "Where are your manners, beast? Don't you know you should bow to the Queen?"

Marco kept his chin firmly up. "You may be the Queen, but I am the King of Beasts."

"You are still an animal. This is my realm, and I rule here now."

"But it's dead! Will you bring the library back to life?"

"Bring the library back for what? A bunch of smelly kids and old men? Libraries, you know, coddle to the lowest common denominator of humanity, and books are a waste of good paper."

"You don't like humans? Or books?" asked Marco, his eyes narrowed. "What are you doing here?"

"Empty buildings are *my* specialty," the Queen breathed, looking fondly at the desolation around her.

"But it wasn't empty until…" How could he reverse the black magic? The Professor had destroyed the library and now this awful creature was challenging him for property rights.

"The Professor did me a huge favor," said the Queen.

None of this made sense to Marco. What was she planning to do?

"And I should thank you for relieving me of the nasty job of getting rid of him. But I won't."

She spoke to something unseen, and a gremlin appeared on the table. He tried to grab the Book but was thrown backwards as the Professor had been, and he high-tailed it back into some dark corner, licking his wounds.

The Queen invited another presence, but nothing as tame as a gremlin. It was some kind of apparition that Marco could only tell was there by following the dark stain it left as it swept over the room. The library was under the control of this mad Queen, and her long robe trailed over the remains of the characters as she tracked the phantom.

A crack in the ceiling split open and the chandelier fell, shattering onto the floor. The Queen watched the phantom spreading its curse and laughed. Alaniah let out a high pitched squeal and curled herself into a cocoon on a top shelf. Lily scrambled to find a hiding place where she could still watch what was happening and Marco, the lion-hearted, began circling the perimeter of the room.

When the phantom appeared to be finished, the Queen turned from the scene as if her job here were done and passed by the mirror. She stopped to admire herself, straightening her crown and smoothing her dress. When she smiled, Marco saw the image in the mirror was not a Queen, but an old hag with black teeth and clouded eyes.

The Queen looked at Marco. She gave a command to a brown lizard that was part of the mirror frame, and it dropped to the floor and scurried towards him, shooting flames with his tongue.

Marco roared, and the lizard burst into flames.

"What fun!" said the Queen. "But I see that was too easy for you, Beast." She waved her wand, and pieces of ceiling drifted down over everything. She called out to the fallen characters still scattered on the floor and they rose and moved towards her in a trance. "What lovely creatures!" she cried out, as they performed a stiff, cardboard-like bow to the Queen. "Come and pay your respects!"

They each took turns walking up to her and she laid her scepter on their shoulders as though knighting them. Then she cackled some welcoming speech to her soulless slaves.

Sparks emanated from along the edges of *The Book of Motion* and the dark festivities were interrupted. In her celebratory moment, the Queen seemed to have forgotten about the Book, which was now hovering above the table, vibrating with light.

"This will not do!" screeched the Queen, as her robe slipped a bit. She ordered one of her minions to fetch the Book and Marco leaped over library tables to reach it at the same time as the dead character. If it weren't for the hat, he wouldn't have recognized who it was. D'Artagnan!

Marco's shock and confusion caused him to hesitate, and the soulless d'Artagnan grabbed the book. Marco tore after him.

The creature dodged tables and chairs, but Marco, now forty times larger than his former self, toppled the furniture in pursuit, which slowed him down considerably.

The Musketeer ran up the stairs and Marco almost had him, until he crawled into a narrow place in the stacks. D'Artagnan, who was not the real d'Artagnan Marco knew, clutched the Book and stared at Marco with dead eyes.

"You can't do anything to an apparition," yelled the Queen from below. "They are under my control."

It was utterly unreal that Marco was faced with attacking d'Artagnan. He stared at the dead gray shell of his hero for a moment. Then he realized that the real d'Artagnan would advise him of nothing less than to go full speed ahead to defend what he'd been given to protect.

Marco smashed his way into the stacks, roaring and knocking apart shelves, which toppled more shelves until all had fallen like giant dominoes. Even the zombie-like d'Artagnan seemed to fear him and he let the Book fall as he made his escape.

A LIFE OF THEIR OWN

Marco returned to the ground floor and bore down on the Queen, roaring and bellowing the words Cicero had given him. "Fa-taw-la-nee!"

As soon as they were out of his mouth the Queen froze, exuding icy calmness. "I've heard rumors about cats guarding the Book, but I do not understand how such a filthy beast can guard something so powerful?"

"I am no rumor," Marco shot back. "I could destroy you in a flash if I chose to."

"Not so easy as you think. I know what you really are," she said, flinging her next words at him like a curse. "You. Are. Nothing!"

Marco answered with a growl.

The Queen kept her distance, pulling her cloak closely around her. "We are the same, you and I. You are not the king of beasts any more than I am Queen. No matter. My followers see me as I desire them to."

Marco roared more ferociously this time, causing the Queen to back off, but only a bit. "You don't scare me. You are just a scrawny housecat!"

"And you? You are a murderer!"

"A murderer?" The hag-queen laughed as she swept her arm in an arc around the room. "I wasn't the one who killed them, but who cares? They didn't deserve their own stories. They were imposters. Not much different than us, don't you think?" Her face contorted in something that was supposed to be a smile. Through blackened teeth, she declared, "And they're all mine now."

Marco growled low, thinking of poor d'Artagnan, whose life was now at the mercy of this demon queen. "Why would they want to follow you?"

"They have no will of their own now." She called out to a boy wearing faded green leotards and a fringed tunic. "What is your name?"

"Peter. Peter Pan."

"Well, Peter, start cleaning up this mess!"

The young boy set about listlessly picking up books off the floor.

"But why destroy the library?" demanded Marco. "Even a hag-queen, such as you, has a story to tell. You could be as famous as Frankenstein or…" He thought there must be a better comparison. "…the Wicked Witch of the West!"

"Ha! I care nothing for silly stories." She looked toward the boy. "Get back to work, Peter!" she ordered the gray boy. He'd stopped cleaning and was reading one of the books.

"What are you going to do with them? They are practically dead!" Marco tried frantically to reason with her.

The Queen waved her wand at them. "I don't know what you mean. I've brought them back to life!"

"They have no life of their own."

"But I'm giving them new life. Come," she said in an overly pleasant manner to a young girl. "What's your name?"

"Ummm… I can't remember," said the girl. She looked a lot like Dorothy from the Wizard of Oz.

"No matter, we will find a new name that suits you," said the Queen. She wrapped her robed arm around the girl and drew her close, like they were old friends.

"See, I can be nice when I want to," she said pointedly to Marco.

Marco growled.

The Queen aimed her scepter at him. "This is my place now. Get out!"

Marco roared louder, but the Queen didn't flinch. "The library is mine! My castle. With the help of my new companions, I can slip into the human's world with no more sound than the moon falling behind a mountain."

The Queen pushed the girl aside and paced the room. "They will not know me, but I will be the one who invades their peaceful dreams." She gazed upwardly as though envisioning the future. "They will not know, but I will be the one who steals their happiness." She stepped up on a chair and laughed. "I will send an army of nightmares to bring them to their knees."

She stood on the table as if that would stake her claim to the realm and looked down upon the wreckage of the library. Marco wondered how it was possible she could see without seeing.

"Fear," she announced triumphantly, "is my greatest weapon!"

The Book of Motion made a strange sound and light leaked out through its pages. The Queen glowered at it. "Get rid of that thing," she ordered Marco.

"You will have to destroy me first," said Marco. "And you can't do that, because I am not afraid of you."

"You're in my way, Beast!" she yelled. She turned to a zombie-gorilla and ordered, "Destroy him!"

The words now came from a deeper place. As the zombies moved to do the Queen's bidding, Marco began to say the words, "Fa-taw-la-nee..."

The Queen drew her scepter.

"...rah-ma-la-nee!" he roared, and the Queen threw daggers from her eyes. She lowered herself to the floor and approached him.

Marco stood stolid as a mountain.

"Ma-fa-la-nee!" he proclaimed, and the Queen unsheathed her scepter, revealing a glowing red sword.

She aimed it towards Marco as he completed the words. "Moon-too-laaaah!" The Queen's sword touched the top of his head, and a surge of pain shot through him.

The Queen brayed like a donkey. Then the dark power went into reverse. Like a giant wave crashing and rolling back onto itself, the Queen's evil power ran backwards through her sword, through her arm and into her body. Her arm withered and her sword clattered to the floor. In slow motion, her body shriveled into a dry carcass, leaving nothing but her crown and robe in a rumpled heap on the floor.

The characters she hadn't turned to zombies were huddled together, ridiculously trying to protect themselves behind a child-sized table. A young girl in a pink tutu began to cry. A clown asked to borrow the woman's fur coat, and then wrapped it around the girl.

Free of her spell, Marco's roar filled the room, terrifying zombies, characters and even Lily. He went to the table where he'd left the Book. He knew what to do. He drew in his breath and blew across the book, cleaning it of any remnants of death and devastation.

Alaniah reappeared, hovering over the Book, wings spread out in full glory. Marco opened the Book and the light blinded everyone.

And the sound… it was painful to his ears, but gradually waves of light and sound receded like the tide going out.

From the mystical world of *The Book of Motion*, the light had done its job. From a book that was more than words, the light overwhelmed the darkness, herding all the demons into their miserable domains and locking the door of their wretched cages.

The library was restored. The first rays of sunlight heightened the colors. A fresh bouquet of yellow tulips appeared on the librarian's desk, the deep reds and browns of old leather, gold and vermillion of a Chinese print. The books were shelved and their characters tucked safely inside. Order reigned.

Then from the stacks, far away at first, the sound of hoofbeats rang through the air. A man on horseback burst from between a set of book shelves and charged across the main floor, miraculously missing tables and chairs. Marco recognized him by his black hat and long white feather.

A light flick of the reins and D'Artagnan's horse slowed to a gentle walk. The Musketeer jumped from his horse and surveyed the library. Then he came over to Marco, whisked off his hat and bowed deeply to the lion.

"Thanks to you Marco, we will live to tell our story another day. I wish you well." D'Artagnan jumped back on his horse. "Godspeed!" he yelled, then galloped back into the stacks.

CAPTAIN OF THE SHIP

Marco surveyed the library from the balcony, the captain of his ship. He loved how window light streamed across tightly-packed rows of books in the late afternoon. There was something appealing as well in the stability of shelved books as the backdrop for the disorder of human activity.

The library had been busier these last few months—ever since rumors of ghosts. At certain times one could hear what sounded like a man talking to himself from underneath the basement-less building. The possibility of encountering a real live ghost attracted young curiosity seekers and they stayed to browse the stacks.

The only report that touched on what had happened came from a trio of teenagers. They swore they'd heard a lion roaring inside the library that night, but everyone laughed at them and none of the other rumors came close to the truth.

He went back to his chambers to check on Lily. The librarians had made a special place for her and their five kittens. Marco figured they wouldn't be contained in the box much longer, and he jumped inside to give a quick wash to a calico, the only one who would sit still.

"I'll be back later," he told Lily. "There's a meeting of the Dead Cats Society tonight."

"What story will you give them, Marco? Will you tell them about turning into a lion?"

"A Guardian never tells his own story, Lily. Tonight Cicero will become part of the legend."

Marco went downstairs and threaded his way through the library, a sort of cat walkabout he liked to take. It was the busiest time of the day. Librarians pushed squeaky book carts. Students, clustered in groups, studied and talked, their conversations punctuated with soft laughter. An old man rattled his newspaper and two silent young boys hunched over a chess board.

He picked his way around backpacks feeling that there was someone he must meet. A familiar voice drew him to a reading corner. Lucy was a regular visitor since her parents had moved in with her grandmother.

She was sitting next to a boy slouched in a chair, both of them lost in their books. When Lucy noticed him, she murmured some greeting and the boy reached one long arm down to scratch his head, his eyes never leaving his book.

The meeting could wait. He nuzzled himself into an impossibly small space and laid his head on the boy's leg. Marco purred. The book was *The Three Musketeers*. D'Artagnan was alive and well.

To find out where Marco appears next, go to:
www.guardiancats.com
www.rahmakrambo.com

Made in the USA
Charleston, SC
16 July 2011